TEXAS SHALL BE FREE!

OTHER BOOKS IN THE
H. BEDFORD-JONES UNIFORM
EDITION LIBRARY:

Abel Smith of Nantucket

Bellegarde

Bowie Knife

Buccaneer Blood

Cyrano

D'Artagnan

The King's Passport

O'Brien, Buccaneer

The Sphinx Emerald

H . BEDFORD-JONES

TEXAS SHALL BE FREE!

H. BEDFORD-JONES

COVER BY
V.E. PYLES

ALTUS PRESS • 2014

First Edition—2014

EDITED AND DESIGNED BY
Matthew Moring

PUBLISHING HISTORY
"Texas Shall Be Free!" originally appeared in the January 4, 11, 18, 25 & February 1, 1936 issues of *Argosy* magazine. Copyright 1936 by The Frank A. Munsey Company. Copyright renewed 1963 and assigned to Steeger Properties, LLC. All Rights Reserved.

THANKS TO
Joel Frieman and Gerd Pircher

TABLE OF CONTENTS

Chapter I 1

Chapter II 13

Chapter III 24

Chapter IV 36

Chapter V 52

Chapter VI 66

Chapter VII 77

Chapter VIII 90

Chapter IX 105

Chapter X 120

Chapter XI 128

Chapter XII 138

Chapter XIII 150

Chapter XIV 159

Some Facts Which Contributed to "Texas Shall Be Free!" . . 176

About the Author 178

CHAPTER I

A MEXICAN DIES

HERE NOW was a man whom it might be ill to cross. That darkly weathered countenance gave warning. The wide-set, sombrous black eyes, seeing all and telling naught; the nose, a very prow with which to cleave danger and difficulties; large straight mouth, supported by a squared chin, itself supported by a bronzed, sinewy neck not easily bent. A strangely powerful face for so meanly garbed a figure!

As Gordon Durant bared his head to the dawn air, his black hair showed curly and close. His figure was erect, lean of waist and thigh, girted about the middle with a leather belt for his sheathed knife. Yet he wore high-peaked straw sombrero, loose faded blue cotton shirt, trousers of like material, and scuffed old brogans. Afoot and thus clad like any peon, he had come ninety miles in three days and nights. Durant of Tennessee, now afoot in the Texas chaparral, and not the only Durant to be braving destiny in these uncertain parts and days of 1836.

He had followed a trail which here dipped into the arroyo. A fitful flow of water, residue of the late rains, gathered in pools. A little farther up the main traveled San Antonio-Goliad road crossed the arroyo by a rude bridge of poles and timbers, which had become undermined at one end so that it was sunk aslant.

The road, such as it was, approximated the north-south course of the San Antonio River, indicated to the westward by a crooked line of green. Durant was headed north for San Antonio, where Travis of the regulars and Bowie of the volun-

"You, hombre!
Come here!"

teers held the old Alamo mission against the thousands of Santa
Anna's Mexicans. Alone, he had come from Goliad, where
Fannin of the Texas Volunteers and four hundred men held the
old mission fort of La Bahia. Bitter word he bore to Travis and
Bowie—word that Fannin's march to relieve them had failed,
word that Mexican armies had spread over the whole southern
part of Texas in a rolling flood designed to stamp out the rebel-
lion of these upstart Americans.

Straight of quick foot like an Indian, Durant climbed the
cut-bank of the arroyo. Beside a scrubby mesquite, he stared
toward the north, where San Antonio and its adjacent Alamo
blended at this distance into one spot of peaceful green nurtured
by flowing waters. What of his destination?

The horizon, brightening in sunrise glow, was scarcely broken.
There was hint of a tower or two, but the morning air hung
breathless to his ear as he listened. There was no shuddering
vibration of gunfire. Was this the peaceful calm of truce, of
victory or defeat, or of sheer weariness? A faint haze seemed
to hover above the city. Smoke of battle, still lingering? Valley

*Durant arose
obediently.*

fog, shrinking before the signals of the sun? Durant shrugged.
Whatever awaited him, he was going in. It was his job. Travis
must get that bitter message, so he might retire before he was
overwhelmed.

Durant turned to swing into the trail—then froze.

A horseman was coming; an officer. The trail, that led into
the highway north of the sunken bridge, was open to view, the
whole road was open, the country was of desert bareness. There
was no hiding, no evasion. Durant had played this game over
ninety miles of enemy country. Now he relaxed, composedly
seated himself beside the mesquite scrub, and under the mush-
room sombrero awaited developments. Drooping eyelids veiled
those sharp, alert black eyes of his.

A captain, this officer. And coming from the south like himself. Bound for San Antonio de Bejar, like himself.

THE MEXICAN was cloaked and booted, his filigreed red képi gleaming like a beacon. He jingled down into the arroyo and eased bridle at the pool. He was swart, mustachioed, soldierly; his eyes flashed to the rim of the arroyo and the man sitting there. Leaving his horse to suck greedily at the pool, he dismounted, took the bridle reins in his left hand, and with his right whipped a pistol from its saddle holster.

"You, *hombre!*" he rapped out. "Come here."

Durant obediently rose and descended into the arroyo again, crossing the stream. His attitude was admirable. He slouched as he walked. A vacuous expression came into his features. He removed his sombrero and ducked his head as he faced the officer.

"Your name, fellow?"

"*Señor*, I am Diego Lopez."

"What are you doing here?"

"I saw your honor coming and waited for you to be first with the pool."

"So? Where are you going?"

"I am from Bejar, *señor*. I am going to join my family at Refugio, below La Bahia, which is known as Goliad."

"You are!" exclaimed the officer. "Then you can tell me how things go in Bejar. I have dispatches for the President, General Santa Anna. The accursed rebels have been whipped out of the Alamo?"

Durant shrugged.

"On the contrary, *señor*, the rebels have been reënforced. They are intent upon recapturing the city; they hold all the roads. I myself got out with difficulty. I would advise your honor to let me guide you in, after dark, by a roundabout path."

The swart face scowled sternly.

"Indeed! And how am I to believe such a story? For Refugio,

eh? Then you have papers vouching for your character, authoriz-
ing you to travel."

"I am only a peon, *señor*," protested Durant. "My papers are
a good pair of legs. No more is required."

The space between the two men had narrowed. Durant stood
deferential but firm, as the officer advanced closer to him.

"Now I know you're lying. You've no pass to leave Bejar. It's
impossible that the rebels should have rallied against five thousand soldiers with cannon. Understand, I am of General Urrea's
staff; we have had couriers from Bejar. I think you're a deserter,
you rascal. You'll not guide me into Bejar, my man; I'll do the
guiding, and take you there at once. Hold out your hands; let
me search you."

With a murmur of humble assent, Durant let his sombrero
drop, extended his arms, and snuffled. He drew back his right
hand to wipe his nose.

SUDDENLY THE dull animal flashed into life. Left hand
seized the pistol barrel. Right hand drove down its edge to the
Mexican's forearm. He tore the pistol from the numbed grip,
and with one savage leap swung the brass-bound butt against
the temple of the officer. It was all done in a single burst of
muscular action.

The blow sounded hollow. With a moan, like a gust of dismay
at death's beck, the Mexican staggered. He fell over sideways
and lay extended, head thrown back and eyes rolling up; then
the lids fluttered and were still. The blue bruise upon his temple
became suffused with blood.

"The devil!" Durant bent above him for an instant, then
straightened and shrugged. "Too hard. Can't be helped now."

He fell rapidly to work, knowing exactly what he was to do.
Time, place and circumstance favored him. He stripped the
limp and lifeless body of its uniform and tossed off his own
humble garb. Swiftly he donned breeches, jacket, boots, cap
and cloak, belted himself with the saber. The uniform might
have been made to his order; anyway, he thus ordered it.

After its first start, the horse stood complacent, fetlock-deep in the cooling water. Durant turned to the saddle, slashed off a thong, and on this hung his sheathed knife safely inside his shirt. Then he glanced at the body, and frowned on the arroyo. No brush here, but plenty by the sunken bridge.

He bundled his own sorry garments into the basket of his sombrero, then stooped and with significant ease shouldered the limp weight of the dead man. He trudged up the arroyo; the horse, pricking its ears and sniffing, followed like a dog.

The bridge was sharply tilted. Screened for half its length by tumbled poles and brush, it provided a handy cache. Durant, bowed with his burden and picking his steps carefully, was nearly there. He was already figuring on where to pitch his load for best disposal, when a cool, amused voice checked him in startled dismay.

"*Viva Dios!* Very well done, my captain! Permit me to assist in the last rites."

From the shadows of the collapsed bridge-end a man sauntered forth, with thin-lipped smile and gleam of wide, horsey teeth. Evidently, he had been all the while sitting under the bridge in close covert.

Durant, still burdened, stood staring.

A lithe, tawny fellow, this, of features round and small, eyes full but hard, nose blunted for flaring nostrils. Feline, alert, dangerous, this face. The man wore costume of bravo or *caballero*, either one; silver-tasseled wool sombrero, white linen shirt, black velvet jacket with tinsel braid, black velvet trousers slashed with yellow, and a yellow sash. Durant caught the outline of a knife. Over arm was a musketoon. From about the bridge-end came the sudden nicker of a horse.

"Surprised, my captain?" The fellow grinned with clenched teeth, like the snarl of a hyena. "You've burden enough on your soul without saddling your shoulders too. Come, we'll chuck him in. Legs to me, arms to you—"

And leaning his musketoon against a sapling, he took hold

and helped ease the burden. With a swing together, they pitched the body up under the bridge, followed it with the sombrero and clothes. Then Durant, grimly amused, eyed his companion inquiringly and met a knowing, leering wink.

"L E T T H E rats say the requiem mass," and the fellow dusted his hands. "We're well met, my good captain. I wasn't sure, at first, it was you. You look more like yourself in that uniform. Whether it's safe or not is for you to say."

Durant's brows lifted. "So you know me, do you?"

The other laughed, and made a curious, swift sign—a circle of thumb and forefinger.

"Do I know you! But I name no names. You're going into Bejar?"

"Unless you aim to stop me."

"The saints forbid! You carry dispatches and are ahead of the news. This dead man won't talk for a day or two. You should have no difficulty with the gold."

"Eh?" Durant frowned, startled. "The gold?"

The fellow tapped his chest, then wiped his throat with quick finger.

"You have three days; El Tuerto waits that long for you to come with the ten thousand yellow boys. Meantime, now that we've picked up your trail you won't escape us again, so play the game and all's well."

All Greek to Durant, but he was far from admitting it. Ten thousand in gold struck at the roots of things. El Tuerto—the One-eyed! And recognition by this cutthroat rascal—why, that could mean only one thing! Durant quivered in every nerve. His nostrils flared, as with a dog on the scent.

"For whom do you take me?" he demanded bluntly, hope-fully.

"For another dead man, if you play false." The thin lips drew back in a snarl. "Why this nonsense? Are you for the gold or not?"

"Of course," said Durant slowly.

"Spoken like a brother, my captain. You really hurt my feelings. We've sat together at monte, and you're none the poorer for it; not to mention that slight affair with the *señorita*—eh?" The rascal grinned. "But we understand each other; no more tricks with Jacopo, I beg of you! I'll arrange all with El Tuerto. Good journey to you, and safe return. To the hilt, brother!"

Again he made the sign of the circle and turned away, but Durant halted him.

"A moment, Jacopo! Are you heading toward Bejar?"

"Away from it, as you well know."

"Well, what's the news there? What of the fighting?"

"All over. You'll smell it when you are there." Jacopo picked up his musketoon. "No Tejanos to bother you; the road's clear. The nearest are at Gonzales, where Santa Anna will gobble them and their general—what's his name? Houston. I hear they declare for independence. *Muy bien!* In war it is the vultures who fatten. Of course I may think you a fool for going into Bejar in uniform—but that's your affair."

Durant's gaze clouded. He wanted to ask more questions, yet dared not chance them. The fighting over? No matter; he must make sure. He had private word for Travis, too.

"By the way," and Jacopo gestured toward the bridge, "the gentleman you killed was Captain Leon de la Vega; well thought of, by all accounts. Naturally I have no eyes nor tongue—but don't delay too long with the gold or I might sprout some. *Adios,* brother of the blade!"

"*Adios,*" said Durant.

Jacopo crossed under the bridge, to where he must have a horse. Durant mounted the animal of the officer and rode down to the trail and out of the arroyo, heading on for the main road and San Antonio de Bejar.

THE SUN was topping the level horizon on his right, flooding all Texas with light. Durant heartily wished that it might illumine the foggy angles in his brain, where fancy groped. However, he had facts enough to busy his wits. Hailed as a "brother of the blade" by a jaunty cutthroat, recognized as a friend and companion, engaged to deliver ten thousand in gold to El Tuerto—no sun was needed to illumine this mystery!

An outlaw clan, of course; freebooters, bandoleros of a sworn company, a brotherhood vowed to loot and to the knife. They might be outlaws from the Gulf coast, deserters from the army, of any and every nation.

"And Jacopo knows me well, eh?" Durant smiled slightly. A mirthless, bitter smile. "That means my information is correct. If he took me for Vincent, then Vincent's in Bejar, and I'll get him. Ten thousand? There is not that much gold in all Texas! It's like that damned Vincent to be in with such a gang. And I thought he was in the Mexican army! So much the better. Gives me more freedom. No message for Travis now, unless I can smuggle Fannin's letter to him. He'll be in jail, I suppose. So much the better for me—find Vincent and kill him, the dirty dog!"

The one purpose rose uppermost in his mind again, where it had lain guiding him these past weeks and months.

The Alamo had surrendered, then; the quiet brooding over the landscape ahead was explained. Smell it? What did that mean? No matter. Better be thinking about himself and his own chances now.

Should he have retained his countryman guise? Diego Lopez might merge with the common herd, unobserved, once inside the town; but now it was no longer a question of getting into the Alamo unseen. An officer with dispatches would be passed without question, and could find Vincent the more readily. But to pose as a staff officer, as Captain de la Vega, who might be well known—hm! Not so good.

Ahead, off the highway, showed the half ruined walls of a mission. Durant reined aside, gained the seclusion of the old walls, and dismounted. He began to examine the contents of his saddle bags.

Traveler's miscellany, a dispatch portfolio; nothing else. No name stamped anywhere. No name in the cap or in the cloak; a few coins in the pockets, a purse as well, but still no name. Good! No papers save a letter to Captain de la Vega, which Durant tore to fragments. Saber and saddle boots—all were clear. But what of the dispatches?

A single letter, fat but sealed, addressed to His Excellency Don Antonio Lopez de Santa Anna. Durant felt his scalp twitching at the name. It had traveled far, this name. Its challenge had brought Davy Crockett and others to the Alamo; had raised the muster from Georgia, Alabama, Tennessee and New Orleans who were at Goliad under Colonel Fannin. Durant felt curious to see this Santa Anna, arch-foe of republican liberty.

But the letter—would it mention the bearer and possibly condemn him as a spy? Durant carefully moistened with his tongue the red wafer sealing the paper together. He wet his knife blade and slipped it through the composition. Presently it came free; no wax seal, luckily! He scanned the slanting script with its flourishes, and the signature of General Jose Urrea. Dated at headquarters, San Patricio, those forty miles from Goliad. No memorandum, no mention anywhere of Captain de la Vega.

SATISFIED, DURANT produced a packet of lucifers from the tunic pocket, and after a moment the heated seal was stuck fast again. He mounted and swung out into the highway again. Time had passed, but it was well worth while. He was secure now, his mind was at ease. His Spanish was fluent, his wits were quick. The long trail was ended, the search was done. Here in San Antonio de Bejar, the damned Vincent would pay for his dastardly act in New Orleans. Then would be time enough to seek out Faith and explain to her. Until then, nose on trail, hand to knife!

"It was like the clever scoundrel to come north with Santa Anna; perhaps he knew I was in Mexico on his trail," reflected Gordon Durant. "Well—attention! There's Bejar."

Touched now by the sun and with clearing details, the city was close. That should be the Alamo, opposite it on the east. By the dust, cavalry or troops must be moving about in the open. The haze, like smoke from spent fires, rested high above the green trees and drab walls, and buzzards circled with exploring eye. The birds of war, to whom all glory is reduced in carrion. No flag appeared over the Alamo.

Country folks were abroad upon the road, and to either side. They respectfully made way for the officer, saluting him with doffed hats as he passed.

Thus Durant passed toward Bejar.

It was the second week of March, 1836.

In Goliad, nearly a hundred miles south, James Fannin and his four hundred men were tempting fate, with General Urrea waiting to close in upon them from San Patricio. Urrea had blood-red bayonets, for he had slaughtered most of Grant's command. Beyond Gonzales in the east, over seventy miles away, Sam Houston was hastening in upon forlorn hope to rally succor for the Alamo, and the new Texas Republic had been proclaimed. In San Antonio the dictator president of Mexico, General Antonio Lopez de Santa Anna, was preparing his five thousand choice troops to sweep the rebellious provinces with fire and no quarter.

Durant, like all outlying Texas, was ignorant of local events, for news was slow to spread. He was spurred by private hatred, private vengeance of the utmost; and if he had some reasonable doubts as to the consequences, he admitted them not nor cared.

So he looked bold-eyed at the horseman now bearing down upon him ahead, smartly cantering but holding his mount in hand as though bound upon a journey. A lieutenant of dragoons, who reined in and saluted brightly.

"*Buenos dias*, captain—God and Liberty! Lieutenant Barras,

with dispatches for the south. You are from San Patricio, perhaps?"

"Yes, with dispatches for His Excellency."

"And you came through without difficulty?"

Durant laughed as he assented, and could breathe more easily.

"And you?" he asked curiously. "I thought there was fighting here?"

The youngster stared at him broadly, then comprehended.

"Of course—you could not know—I'm the first out with the word. Yes, all was well settled here. *Dios!* What a hell it was!" He sobered momentarily, then tightened rein. "I must be on. I trust you bring His Excellency good news, for you'll find him in bad humor."

"After victory? How is that?"

"The cursed Alamo cost him five hundred men and more. *Adios!*" With wave of hand, the lieutenant rode on.

"Five hundred—whew!" Durant whistled softly. "Why, Travis had only a hundred and eighty all told!"

He went his way, until destiny overtook him with scurvy hand.

CHAPTER II

THE NEW NAPOLEON

THE CITY lay close ahead. To right and left crowded green irrigated fields, high trees, farmsteads. Durant had heard the clatter of hooves to rear, but he did not turn to look as uneasy conscience might bid.

He waited until the moment was ripe and glanced aside, to see a *ranchero* upon a long-legged mule. The mule, blown and rebellious, readily yielded to the rein, slackening pace to match that of the horse. The rider was a small wizened man wearing a huge hat and enormous spurs. He uttered breathless, excited salutation.

"God and Liberty! You are for Bejar, *senor?*"

"If I am, then what?" Durant parried.

"I would ride in with you," the other panted. "It is a military matter. You're an officer. You can be of great help to me."

Durant's pulses failed for an instant. He knew what was coming, guessed it.

"What is the matter you mention?"

"A dead man, *senor*. There is a body under the Arroyo Hondo bridge, back some miles on this very road," the other wheezed. "Murder has been done, *senor!* I'm going into Bejar to report it."

"You saw the body?" demanded Durant sternly.

"I did indeed," and the *ranchero* hastily crossed himself, with a slight shiver. "I have a small *rancho, senor*. I left early to look for some cows that had strayed. Owing to the state of the country, this old mule is the only saddle animal I have left. When I rode into the arroyo I happened to look about under the bridge and saw a terrible thing. A corpse tucked away, *señor!* Not long dead; the flies and rats had not found it. But the head was bloody, and the body was stripped. Near by was a bundle of common clothes. I think someone traded clothes with the dead man. So I left word at my house, and here I am."

"Very bad, certainly," commented Durant. "But why do you say a military matter?"

"It is so." The little man wiped sweat from his eyes. "I go not to the alcalde but to the camp. The murdered man was an officer in the army; I even know his name, for I have seen him before. He has stopped at my house. He is known hereabouts. A great *caballero*, not a Mexican but a *caballero* of Spain."

Durant swallowed hard. His quick, hard eyes found no guile in the little rancher.

"And you wish to go into the city with me, then?"

"But yes, if you will permit. You will know how to take me to His Excellency, the general and president, the great soldier, Santa Anna! I am a poor man and have need of the reward. His Excellency will be generous after his great victory here. The dead man was Captain Leon de la Vega. Perhaps you, *señor*, knew him?"

"I have heard the name," Durant said. "Come along, then."

There was no way out of it, no way to shake off this fellow who was like a burr. What a devilish stroke of luck! Durant could not let him get into Bejar first, with his news for the authorities; nor could he prevent his getting there, for the road was open, the mule had legs, the man had definite aim.

"It is for His Excellency in person," insisted the little man. "A thousand thanks to you, *señor!* You may be rewarded too— who knows?"

Durant gave moody ear to the prattle, inwardly cursing the rancher. This greedy fellow running with his news promised to sharpen the eyes of all Bejar for strangers in uniform.

THEY WERE coming into the city by the Goliad road from the southeast; thus the old Alamo lay fair to the right. Durant eyed it as Colonel Fannin had described the place to him. A large walled yard, a two-story chapel, upon a rise of the plain across the river from the town. The plain was a humming camp arrayed in careless security.

The road took on the aspect of an outflung street. There would be a ford or bridge at the river; a beaten road cut across northward, as though for the Alamo.

"*Viva!* A noble sight, this city!" bleated the rancher. "One would not think such a battle had just taken place. And where do we find His Excellency, *señor?*"

Durant drew rein, and the mule halted at his stirrup.

"Listen, *mi amigo,*" he said confidentially. "One does not see *El Presidente* at the drop of a hat, without arrangement. If he's occupied we might have to cool our heels for some time. And I have important business for his immediate attention, since I bear urgent dispatches. Have you anywhere in the town you can remain?"

"But certainly, *señor.* The house of my cousin, Don Angel Prieto."

Durant nodded. He had the game in hand now. All he needed was half an hour.

"Good. Then keep on across the river here, where there'll be no soldiers to question you. Breathe not a word of what you know to any soul here, or the news will be stale before you reach His Excellency. Meantime, I'll arrange with him to receive you as soon as possible."

"You'll tell no one?"

"Trust me for that!" and Durant laughed. "I'd gain nothing, for I found no body. And I've my own affairs to look after. Tell me where to send for you."

"Yes; I'll be waiting," the little man eagerly replied. "The name is Pedro Ortiz, at the house of Angel Prieto in Santa Maria Street."

"And mind, keep your mouth shut, or the civil authorities will be after you for concealing a crime!" Durant cautioned him. "You must await the pleasure of His Excellency. I'll send for you."

"Agreed, *señor*, and a thousand thanks!"

Full of importance, Pedro Ortiz jabbed his mule and hurried along.

Durant turned into the beaten road trending north, with the river and city to his left. No delivering those dispatches now; that was needless risk, with this bleating rascal ready to spill word of murder. No, he must seek a tavern or wine-shop, merge with other men in uniform, lose himself and his identity for another less risky. Any place would do, where he might lie perdu until darkness fell. He needed sleep, also. He could well sleep the day away.

And with darkness—nose to trail, hand to knife! The mocking laughter of Vincent beckoned him on, and his black eyes hardened on the road.

This forked—one way for town, across a bridge, and the other way to the Alamo. And here at the fork, unexpectedly, half a dozen soldiers came slouching out of the shade to block his way, with a trim young officer in spruce command. An outpost guard, stationed here to examine incomers. Again Durant stifled a curse and drew rein, his eyes probing sharply.

"YOU ARE from the outside, *señor?*" said the officer politely. "Your name and business, if you please. Orders."

Boldness was the only answer. Durant spoke with quick authority.

"From General Urrea, with dispatches for His Excellency in the city. Let me pass, *señor*."

"Impossible, captain; a thousand apologies," and the officer smiled. "It is necessary that you first report to General Filisola, second in command. Those are my orders for all dispatch bearers. The general is quartered at the Alamo. I'll escort you to him myself, with your permission."

The only answer lay in soldierly obedience. Durant forced down his chagrin; things were not going to his taste, but could not be helped. After all, he could deliver his dispatches, make the best of matters, then disappear in the city.

The officer mounted and rode beside him, chatting agreeably. Durant's attention, however, was fixed upon the fortress and its approaches. Fire and shot and shell had been at work here. The plain was scarred, walls had been blazed with lead and iron, cannon embrasures were blackened by powder fumes, parapets were chipped and crumbled. The chapel rose gaunt and ragged, its window openings mutely staring as though blanked by horror. Soldiers were toiling to repair damages.

A peculiar scent, acrid, rank, as of charred and smoldering rubbish, pervaded the air. Durant recollected the words of Jacopo: "You'll smell it when you're there." A queer sensation seized upon him, a hesitancy to ask questions. The officer noticed his manner, and made light comment.

"I see you're interested; it is natural. Your first view of the ground? *Dios!* You should have been here on the day itself!"

"The place was taken by assault, then? I see the soldiers clearing away ladders."

"Bah! Those devils made short work of men and ladders. We had to enter by a breach choked with our own dead. Three, times we tried, and then—" The officer spread out his hands significantly. "I need say no more. Victory, to sweeten breakfast!"

"So they surrendered, eh?" said Durant.

The other blinked at him. "What's that? I forget; you just arrived. They were rebels in arms, they refused to surrender at discretion—why, damn it, they set out to shoot everybody within range! So we carried no terms except ball and bayonet, when we finally went in. They resisted until the last man went down."

"The devil!" Durant exclaimed. He was slow to comprehend what was told him, what was implied. "You mean that few prisoners were taken? But some of them must have escaped or fled?"

The other laughed harshly.

"Not one, *caballero*; not one! Their souls are all roasting in hell, as their bodies roasted here. You see, when the affair was over, His Excellency directed an auto-da-fé for the carcasses as an expression of contempt. They made three piles of wood and flesh. You can see one of the ash-heaps yonder. *Caspita!*" The officer wrinkled his nose. "I'll never get the stench out of my nostrils. The taint seems to linger in the air, in the trees, in the very ground itself."

Gusts of horror beat at Durant's brain. He could find no words for utterance.

For a moment of imagination the plain erupted a dragon's-teeth crop of bayonets moving forward in serried ranks. The Alamo was veiled in battle smoke rent by cannon gushes and rifle spurts. Travis, Bowie, Crockett and the others; all ashes now. Cold rage, infinite compassion, glorying pride of blood, fought each other within Durant's mind and clogged his tongue. Momentarily he forgot even Vincent and the driving power that had fetched him here.

THEY ENTERED the Alamo inclosure. The yard interior was still littered with bursts of iron, pitted with shell holes. Walls were splashed with rusty red. Durant was aware of men and officers, of gold braid, of eager tongues, yet could see nothing except that vision of brave men dead and burned. Then a word pierced to him.

"General Don Vicente Filisola! Dispatches for His Excellency, my general."

Vicente! The name was all too familiar; fortune seemed to be playing a game upon the word. Here before his clearing gaze was not the Vincent he knew, not the Vincent of a day past and a day to come, not Vincent Durant at all. General Vicente Filisola was plainly enough an Italian. Darkly olive with black side-whiskers, a mat of closely curling hair, intelligent, glowing eyes. Aides and messengers around him, the escort officer waiting at attention. Durant came out of the saddle and saluted.

A moment of sharp scrutiny was broken by a sudden smile, an extended hand.

"That is good. You are from—"

"General Urrea, sir."

"Your name?" queried the general.

Durant was awake now, alive to danger, swift to impromptu decision.

"Captain Ramon Segura, sir."

"Of the Tampico Battalion, I see." Confound the man, how did he see? "You will kindly deliver your dispatches to me; they'll be forwarded at once. His Excellency will receive you in person as soon as possible, I'm sure."

"The dispatches are here in my saddle bags—"

"No. Wait, *señor*—"

Filisola made a sharp gesture and leaned aside; an aide was whispering at his ear. His brows lifted in astonishment; his eyes dwelt again upon Durant.

"Impossible!" ejaculated the general under his breath. Then he stroked his whiskers, as the aide stepped back.

Tension gripped Durant suddenly. What was wrong? The warning chill clutched at him. If aught had gone amiss, he was now a lost man; no boldness, no swift stroke, could extricate him. Then the brow of Filisola cleared and he spoke again, brusquely and yet affably.

"On second thought, Captain Segura, you had best deliver your dispatches into the hands of His Excellency. They may be of utmost importance, and it would ill become me to cheat you of due honor. Lieutenant! A fitting escort, six men; you yourself will ride over with the captain. I'll send word ahead, so that he may be received without delay. His Excellency will assuredly be pleased to see you. One of you gentlemen ride with word to headquarters. Dispatches from General Urrea at last."

The smile of Filisola was quizzical, cordial, more in seeming than in substance. Durant's apprehension lifted, however, at these last words. An aide clattered away, the lieutenant ordered up six troopers for escort. Filisola shook hands heartily and saluted again as he turned away.

Yet something was wrong. As Durant rode off toward the city with his escort, he felt a tightening of events. He was perhaps accused of—what? Impossible to say. Not of killing anyone, not of playing the spy, or he would have been seized without ceremony. He seemed to have roused astonishment, rather than hostility.

Well, see it through! All depended now on closing the interview with Santa Anna and getting dismissal, while Pedro Ortiz waited at the house of Angel Prieto. How long the fellow would wait, was the question. Durant knew that he himself would be assigned to quarters; the dispatches might require an answer; he must plead for an immediate return. Once beyond sight, he could duck for cover.

AGAIN HE cursed the net of circumstances around him. His private errand here with Vincent Durant must mark time. Things were not going to schedule. The body under the bridge was a vague menace; the officious Pedro Ortiz was sharper peril. He dared not keep to this guise of Captain Ramon Segura a moment longer than necessary, either.

Every man in the Alamo killed, without quarter, the bodies burned in contempt! The picture blazed in his brain like the flames of the funeral pyres themselves. Fannin must learn of this. Houston must learn. The settlements, all Texas, must learn of it! Not even the wounded spared. Slaughter, without mercy!

The horses were clattering through the streets of the town now, bravely decked out as though for a fiesta. There was the plaza ahead, and the palace of the governor; now headquarters, as the sentries testified, and the fine horses at the hitch-rack in front. Durant dismounted with his escort, took the sealed dispatch from his saddle bags, and tramped in amid clanking sabers and rattling spurs.

And so, to the presence of the great man, the conqueror, the new Napoleon. He was resplendent, seated stiffly at a polished mahogany table, and surrounded by uniforms only less decorated than his own, so that they beamed as by reflected light.

A man slight of frame, making the most of his inches by military erectness and uniform collar to his ears. A man of long, smoothly shaved countenance, Creole in tint, strongly marked. Impatient, intolerant, cruel, weak, a vein of passion in the high forehead—such was Santa Anna, Dictator of Mexico.

In his instant of thus appraising the butcher of the Alamo, Durant sensed that he himself stood alone in a very narrow trail whose next turn led—whither? He could not foresee. It was sentineled by Fate. But there were other signs, weather signs. Dark eyes intent upon him, haughty, amused, piercing.

Santa Anna was in a bad humor, as predicted. His gaze, sweeping Durant from head to foot, announced ready thunder and lightning. He vented curt demand:

"From General Urrea? Your dispatches."

Durant handed over the dispatch. Santa Anna examined the address, slashed the seal with poniard paper-knife, and fastened upon the contents of the packet. His face cleared, and he relaxed. Watching him, Durant breathed more easily.

"Gentlemen," exclaimed *El Presidente* to his officers, "the worthy General Urrea has destroyed the rebels under Colonel Grant and is secure in San Patricio. He will march upon Refugio, and thence dispose of the principal rebel nest at Goliad, formerly La Bahia, where the pirates and filibusterers under the traitor Fannin are fortified. God and Liberty! This little war of ours is practically over. Rebels in arms now know what fate awaits them. If that fellow Houston is somewhere in the bush, we'll smoke him out and burn every cluster of American huts in Texas."

Amid murmurs of assent and adulation, Santa Anna tossed

the dispatch aside. He looked on Durant again—and the room suddenly chilled. His voice leaped out with a soft note of feline anger. A deadly note.

"So! You are Captain Segura, eh?"

Durant saluted. "Yes, Your Excellency."

El Presidente played upon the word, with thin smile.

"Segura! *Segura*—yes, you certainly are 'assured,' my good captain. Segura, and of the Tampico Battalion by the evidence of your uniform."

DURANT'S HEART sank. In the words, in the voice, in the black darting eyes, he read that he was meshed in some accursed net which he could not comprehend. He recalled the grinning astonishment of Jacopo that he should be going to San Antonio. Then, of a sudden, Santa Anna's smile was wiped away by a violent explosion of words.

"*Santo Dios!* I never heard of such effrontery. You actually exhibit yourself in this city, you dare to come to my headquarters! It is incredible, unless you were drunk; yet you are certainly sober. How you came by these dispatches in the service of General Urrea, I don't know; but it shall be found out. There'll be time enough."

Thin fist pounded the table. "You damned insulting scoundrel! You treacherous dog!" cried out Santa Anna, convulsed with fury that darkened his swart cheeks. "You shall be stripped of that uniform! You shall make answer—but not here, not here. By the nails of Christ, one word from you and I'll have you flogged to death! Here, you," and the general beckoned an officer. "Take him away, lock him up like the common criminal he is. The council of war shall deal with him."

A quick movement around, a firm hand upon Durant's shoulder, the curt order: "Your sword, *señor!*"

His cloak was snatched away. Belt and scabbard, loosed from his waist, slithered to the floor. Durant thought of the knife inside his shirt, against his skin; he shut it desperately from his mind lest the thought betray him. The knife in its beaded sheath had values of the greatest, but never greater promise than now.

Somehow, somewhere, he was trapped and caught; he could not see how or where. What a fool he had been, to challenge this venture! To voice his anger was useless. The charge against him, whatever it was, appeared to be something of common knowledge, yet outside his own ken. If he forced the issue, he might make a bad matter worse.

Tongue bridled, brain in a groping moil, he submitted to being marched out of the room, out of the corridors, out again into the blinding white sunlight of morning. He drew a deep breath. Bewilderment passed. His shoulders squared back and the lines of his face tightened.

If the present were despair, there remained the future!

CHAPTER III

ANOTHER MAN'S SHOES

G UARDS CLOSED about him and he was headed across the open plaza.

Soldiers and civilians gave way to the hurrying squad, and then pursued it with curious stares. Durant strode on, unbound but secure. The city was all strange to him, the buildings unaccustomed, the people unknown. He had been down through Mexico and up north again, always with nose to trail, with hand to knife, following the unholy scent of Vincent Durant; but here he was in new territory. Then he caught a look, a face, a gesture.

A young woman in yellow skirt, with lacy black mantilla draping her from head to waist, stepped aside from the path of the squad. She stopped short, and as he was hustled past, Durant met lustrous eyes directed full upon him from that lacy canopy, two stars shining from a moon-rifted cloud. The eyes widened with startled recognition, amazement and shocked wonder.

Then, impulsively, she drew her shawl closer about her face and turned away with sway of hips. To Durant remained an agreeable vision of a small, piquant face, soft red lips, short uptilted nose, and those compelling eyes of starry midnight under black brows etched against white skin.

"A pretty baggage for somebody's pack," grunted a soldier of the squad.

"She is for your betters; keep silent," ordered his corporal.

"Well, a man is a man," retorted the soldier. "And a woman's a woman."

Durant visioned his prison ahead. A two-story barracks, and in the rear of this, a low row of adobe rooms. His cell was at the far end of this row. As they came to it and the door was flung open, Durante held back, looked at the officer beside him.

"Can you tell me what charge is laid against me?"

The officer stared into his eyes, then broke out with hearty laughter.

"Come, come, that's a good one! I charge you with being a fool. Hang it, I did envy you the luck you had, but this appearance of yours shows that the devil traded it to you for your wits. And now that I've answered you, suppose you tell me the name of that fair black-eyes who certainly knew you."

"I never saw her before," Durant said.

The officer snorted at this. "So! Then she'll be an old woman before you see her again. All right, men! Clap him in."

Durant was shoved in. The heavy door was slammed and bolted.

His luck? What did the man mean? Bewilderment closed in upon him. Clearly, he was the subject of amusement to all around. He took stock of his prison. Dusty pallet, leather-seated stool too light for a weapon, entrance door, blank thick partition walls of the drab flinty clay, the outer wall pierced six feet up with a square opening, barred, ample for ventilation. Outside he could hear the shuffling steps of a guard.

He sank down upon the stool, head in hands. So far, it was evident that he was charged with no capital crime. The sarcastic dictum of Santa Anna, the banter of the officer, proved this much. But what was forthcoming? When he thought upon Pedro Ortiz, bursting with zeal and greed, apprehension chilled him. He could stand no investigation.

That dead body under the bridge would be found. General Urrea would be queried. He must get free of these walls before the storm broke. Much depended on how long Pedro Ortiz would wait with his secret, in hope of audience and fitting reward. Durant rather guessed the little man would wait some time, and then would have difficulty in reaching the general. But—damnation! The vision rose clearer of a wall and a firing squad. Spy! Well, a man had to risk that end, in taking on such a venture, but Durant disliked having it thrust upon him by a trick of fate.

TIME PASSED, as he brooded and fidgeted. Sounds filtered in to him; bugle notes, the jangle and hubbub of the barracks, the stir of the guard outside, echoes of more distant life in street and plaza. He was constantly on edge for a peremptory summons. "There'll be plenty of time," Santa Anna had said.

"I hope to Heaven he's right!" muttered Durant.

The hot hours waxed and waned; noon came and passed, he remained incommunicado. Flogged to death—for what? The mystery of it was torture. Some mistake, no doubt; some little thing that might have been explained away. Or it might not. Durant paced up and down his cell, tormented by uncertainty, by a thousand possibilities. And yet, oddly enough, the truth never once came into his mind.

The dusty afternoon died at last. He wakened to sunset, realized that he had been stretched out, asleep, on the pallet. Voices outside his window, harsh commands; the guard was being changed. The bolts of his door were shot back.

Durant, on his feet now, swung around. A soldier passed in a basin of stew, a jug of water, then straightened up and grinned at him. Glittery, reptilian eyes, unshaven swart face—then a hand uplifted, making the circle sign of thumb and forefinger.

"All is well, brother!" said the soldier. "Remember your oath. Have patience! The iron is weak."

He was gone again, the door slammed, the bolts shot home. And upon Durant, all astare and astounded, burst the truth.

"Brother" again, and the sign of the circle! This brotherhood had parts, assuredly. It had been "brother" under the bridge, when Jacopo had mistaken him for that rascally Vincent—Vincent—Vincent Durant! Why, there was the secret of the whole thing—there was the damned reason behind this embroglio!

As Vincent, he had amazed Jacopo, General Filisola, the officers. As Vincent, he had provoked the wrath of Santa Anna. Why? What had Vincent further committed, beyond engaging to deliver ten thousand in gold to El Tuerto and thus avoiding a slit throat? Well, time would tell.

There was the answer! Once more he was mistaken for Vincent, this accursed half-brother of his; yes, he might have known it. Vincent, in Mexican service, had been guilty of some scoundrelly action—as usual. Here, as in New Orleans, as elsewhere, the one brother had been mistaken for the other, and small blame for the error. They were alike, save for slightly shorter stature, a flare of deviltry in the black eyes, a blacker heart; alike, save for dishonor and the wages of hell.

And alike in the bitter hatred each bore the other.

So this explained everything! Durant threw back his head and laughed, laughed in unassumed relief. Now that he knew the worst, he could cope with it. The worst? Perhaps the best! For he had not missed that sign of thumb and finger. Now, as "brother" again, he would get out of this, with purpose unquenched—nose to trail, hand to knife! He touched the flat sheath inside his shirt.

DUSK DRIFTED in through the window opening; the twilight in the room swiftly faded. What was it the soldier had said about the iron being weak? Durant caught at the recollection and went to the window.

He tried the bars there. One of them gave a little to his exploring fingers. Have patience—for what, for how long? He turned away from the window, and the scuff of his boots on the earthen floor maddened him. The thought of Pedro Ortiz prodded him. The bars of the window drew at him, and his fingers itched. Patience? Only until the barracks quieted, then.

The inviting darkness thickened outside. A voice pricked at him, a cautious voice from outside, below the window.

"Vicente! Do you hear?" The words were carried upon the muted alto of a woman. "Vicente!"

"Yes, yes!" He pressed to the window. "What is it?"

"Why did you come back? Why have they put you in jail?"

"I don't know."

"It does not matter; we shall go together. The guard is friendly. You must get out at once."

"Gladly, gladly!" and Durant laughed a little. "But how?"

"A bar is loose in the window. You can dig around it. *Dios!* If I only had a knife to give you!"

"I have a knife," he cut in.

"Good! Pick the bar free, then. Everything is ready. I am waiting for you."

Durant reached inside his shirt. A woman—Vicente, eh? Not the officers alone had recognized him; perhaps this was the same black-eyes whom he had met in the plaza. So Vincent was up to his old tricks with the girls! Well, this time the affair held a certain grim humor. This time, his likeness to Vincent was helping him out of a bad hole—would help him to the throat of that devil in guise of man!

The barracks had quieted. There came no sound, save a hasty breathing outside the window. Durant pulled up the stool, unsheathed his knife; standing on the uncertain footing, he pricked about the bar, socketed in the clay casement.

After all, it was absurdly simple, once given the cue.

The bar yielded. Water had softened the hard adobe—no doubt, while he had been asleep. Yes, this brotherhood certainly had its value! With a grim chuckle, Durant tore the bar loose at the bottom; the clay at the top came away in chunks. The sound of their fall drew no attention. Using the bar as a lever, he attacked the second bar. This, too, had been wet down, and the first bar forced it from the socket. He lowered both bars to the cell floor, gained the stool again, drew himself up to the window.

Clutching fingers, a heave of his body, and he was squeezing through the frame. With a twist and a scramble, he let himself slide outward, fell to the ground, lurched to hands and knees, then gained his feet.

A DARK cloaked shape materialized beside him. Warm hands clasped him; warm lips sought his in eager embrace. Nor did he refuse.

"Thanks be to God!" came the low words. "Here is a cloak for you, *mi corazon!*"

My heart! The face, so close, was that of the young woman in the plaza. Durant hesitated, repugnant to play the part; then she went on swiftly.

"I have horses ready, Vicente. Come! We cannot talk here. Follow me—give me your arm, rather. The house is not far, as you should know."

Durant fastened the cloak that fell about his shoulders. She took his arm, laughing a little under her breath, excitedly. They walked away openly, sedately, from the barracks row, and came presently to a narrow street.

And Durant came to decision. He was taken for Vincent—very well! Once, back in New Orleans, Vincent had played the part of Gordon Durant to shame and dishonor. That had been under cover of the stars, also; with darkness to aid, the girl who loved Gordon Durant had failed to discover the cheat and fraud.

"Good! I'll play Vincent now—but not to dishonor," thought Durant. "To freedom. To get nose on trail again, hound him down, kill him as I've sworn. Will this Spanish girl detect the fraud? Perhaps. If so, she shall have the truth."

A pressure on his arm, a word. He was whisked through a gateway into a private courtyard, where two saddled horses idly mouthed their bits. Then the girl beside him spoke softly, intimately.

"The leather case is still where we put it, Vicente. When I

saw you there in the plaza, under arrest—ah! It was terrible. Santa Anna ordered it. Does he know?"

"Bah! What could he know?" Durant evaded.

"If he suspected that we were going away together, and taking the casket—you told nobody, Vicente? Nobody?"

"Upon my honor," said Durant, "I have not mentioned it to a soul."

"Good! Then let him suspect, let him search! He'll never get it now." Her voice steadied in a passionate resolution. "Lucky that you have friends, Vicente! The soldier spoke to me, told me what to do. My father has not arrived yet; I had no trouble. But come along—you can carry the leather case for me. We'll get it and go."

She drew him away into the house, with tap-tap of urgent heels.

Durant swallowed hard, but held to his decision. What it was all about he had not the faintest idea—except that Vincent Durant had been up to his usual deviltry. He did not so much as know her name, and dared not ask it. He liked her air of capability, however, and the fresh, sweet perfume that floated in her wake.

They were in a dark hallway; she halted him near a dim lamp burning in a niche. She briefly fumbled at the wall. There was a click, then she laughed with a note of triumph. With the gleam of her white face again, and the gesture of her extended hands, Durant found himself holding a flat, heavy weight. A leather case or casket, cased in canvas.

THE CATCH of the hiding place clicked. The girl, breathing warmth and eagerness, was again in motion. "It is heavy, heavier than I thought! Well, I have the key. You shall make it fast behind your saddle, Vicente." Her low laugh rippled again. "Santa Anna will never get the jewels of Amadora de la Vega for his war fund! Let him go and rob elsewhere. Even Captain Don Leon, my uncle, will approve of this when he hears."

The words struck Durant in the face like the blow of a whip, flung back as she led the way outside again. Amadora de la Vega—that was her name, then. Doña Amadora. And Captain Leon de la Vega was, or had been, her uncle. The body of the good captain still lay under the bridge. The thought of Pedro Ortiz came recurrent.

Somehow, blindly stumbling under the weight in his arms and the weight in his brain, Durant was out in the courtyard with her. He was bewildered, dazed by what he had just learned. It seemed fantastic and unreal.

What did the casket hold, then—jewels, as she had said? Strange; all of forty pounds weight in this leather case. He was beside the horse now. Pistols in the saddle boots. He cradled the burden in the poncho roll behind the saddle; by report of fingers and eyes, the canvas wrapping was fastened by laced thongs. He secured it in place. If he were playing Vincent's part now, well and good! Play it out, see whither it led him. Get to the bottom of all this mixup before he put hand to knife again. That was plain common sense. The trail might lead him to the kill as well as another.

He handed the *doña* to her own saddle, and swung up. She wheeled for the gate. The night had thickened. Save for errant noises from liquor shops, where soldiers and civilians gathered, these precincts of the town lay silent, with never a challenge of the gently pacing hooves.

Durant let the woman slant their course, which led through byways and dark streets. She knew the town, he did not. She spoke not. His horse pressed along with hers on loose rein, his senses probing the obscurity around.

Then, almost before he could realize it was true, they were on the outskirts of town. They plashed through a stream. Some unguarded ford of the river itself, Durant judged. Now they were in the open, sparsely broken by huts, and were hailed by barking dogs. She swung sharply aside into the open murk of a field, and then her mount was reined in. A traveled road was before them.

"Heaven be thanked, we're out!" Relief, tension relaxed, spoke in her voice. "Isn't this the Bahia road, Vicente? But we can't keep to it. If there's pursuit, if they seek us, they will look in the south. I think we should make east, at least until morning. Toward Gonzales, eh? But you decide. My work's done, and you know best of this matter."

"The east, by all means," Durant said. "And Gonzales."

"Very well; turn left into the Gonzales road, a little way on." She gathered up her reins, and her little laugh rang uncertainly. "We can turn off for the south again, in the morning. The Texans are in the east, in Gonzales itself. They'll not like your uniform when they hear about the Alamo! It is of the Tampico Battalion, like that of my uncle. Ah!" She sniffed the night air. "It is horrible; it will never clear. I shan't forget until we're in Cuba."

THE ALAMO, then! To Durant it seemed that her subtle perfume failed to counter the whiff of stale human ashes clinging to his nostrils, permeating the very air. He pricked his horse on. If this were the Goliad road, as she said, they must head left to reach Gonzales. Well, why not? Best let Vincent wait, let the knife stay cool till he learned the truth behind all this.

"Very well, head east," he said.

Gonzales was seventy miles away. Goliad might have been already taken; the Urrea dispatch had been ominous.

Her voice reached him again, broke through his thoughts, as they cantered on.

"We'll go to Cuba together, my Vicente! When we reach the coast we can find a ship for New Orleans. Did you hear about the victories? We need not worry about the Texans; General Urrea is attending to them. Still, I wish you did not have that uniform, Vicente! I did not know you were of my uncle's regiment; why did you never tell me?"

Durant smiled under the misty stars.

"True, I never thought to mention it," he said. He did not need to give great heed to his words. She was paying more attention to her own, to her thoughts, than to what he murmured.

"We'll turn south at dawn, yes," she was saying. "We'll join my uncle in San Patricio and be safe there. And there'll be good people to help us on our way, Vicente. Tomorrow we can stop at the Ortiz *rancho*. Pedro Ortiz is a cousin of Angel Prieto, you know. Señor Prieto, my good friend, told us that Señor Ortiz would send us on—"

Again her words hit like a blow, provoking amazement, an insane desire to burst into raucous laughter. The names lashed home. Was there no escape from that dead man under the bridge? Or his accursed uniform of the Tampico Battalion?

They found the Gonzales road and jogged along, hour upon hour, cloaked against the thin mist and the cold night.

Doña Amadora chattered, and the details came forth, but not the details Durant most wanted to hear. She knew nothing of the reason for his arrest.

Otherwise, the situation assumed shape, in some respects, and Durant could assort the facts.

Vincent—that whelp Vincent again!—and this pretty *doña* were appointed to make off for the Gulf and New Orleans and thence to Cuba, taking the Vega jewels, to save them from the war levy of *El Presidente*. No doubt, to preserve them for the war levy of Vincent Durant, who had been in the Mexican service, and who certainly was the lover of Doña Amadora. She anticipated great happiness with her Vincent in Cuba; she prattled of it as she rode, and wakened from dozing to prattle anew.

Gordon Durant knew her Vincent better than she did, and had his own notions. He himself was not going to the Gulf, not going to the south at all, and still less to the *rancho* of Pedro Ortiz.

No. He owed her a debt, and he would pay it. Save her from that devil Vincent, place her in safety with her jewels at Gonzales, tell her the truth about the man she loved, the bitter truth, and prove it. This must be his errand now; play the man's part. The vengeance trail had forked. If he could save her, and those jewels behind his saddle, from the devil's claws of Vincent, he should do so.

And what of Vincent, then? Well, if he had missed rendez-vous with the *doña*, he might still turn up in San Antonio. Apparently he had not been there after all, or had been there and departed, to come again. In which case, honest Vincent might find himself in a pickle, might be taken for the Captain Segura of the dispatches. Durant's lips curved bitterly at the thought. No such luck! That crafty devil was too smart.

O N A N D on they rode, Durant talking little. They made brief halts; to breathe the horses, to water them, to stretch limbs while Durant tightened girths, to readjust the heavy chest behind his saddle. Once, sinking to the ground with a little sigh, the *doña* had slept for a few brief minutes, leaned within his arm; relaxed there, soft and fragrant as a flower, while the breath from her parted lips fanned his cheek. Durant had small allure of her. Another woman—the other woman—lingered against his background of life with harsh and false accusation. That, too, must wait until the vengeance trail was reddened and ended.

So the long night passed, and the miles drifted behind with the stars.

"We will go into the south soon, Vicente?"

She was growing uneasy now, vexed at his dark silence, his lack of attention, his continual following of the road. The chap-arral had lightened a little, the air was deep and chill with the night's dew, as they rode onward into the dawn.

"You're in uniform, remember; we must not keep on too far, Vicente! There will be Texans ahead. They are terrible, these Tejanos."

"They're in Gonzales, not here," Durant said, to quiet her. "We're nowhere near Gonzales, Doña Amadora. It's too soon to turn southward; we must await a trail, and the daylight."

Then, at last, sky and earth were bright with the rising sun. The road behind lay all clear of pursuit. The road ahead dipped below a rise veiled with chaparral, and they rode on into the unknown. The trail wended on down and down again into a brushy swale pungent with the greening tips of spring—the desert miracle.

"*Dios mio!* Your pistols, Vicente!" burst forth the girl suddenly, turning a tragic face to him, a face large-eyed and wearily appealing. "No, we are lost—"

Durant's eyes narrowed, but he made no move for the weapons. A man with barring rifle had appeared in the road ahead. To right and left two mounted men crashed through the brush. Doña Amadora, now white and defiant, sat her saddle stiffly.

Texans, by the grace of God! Durant relaxed, drew a deep breath. His present problem seemed to be solved; until he caught the gaze of the girl turned to him, her dark eyes widened with terror. He could imagine the thought unuttered: "Your uniform, Vicente!"

Again, that accursed uniform of the Tampico Battalion.

CHAPTER IV

HARSH WELCOME

THEY SAT there in the sunrise, unmoving, Durant and the *doña*. To either hand, a mounted Texan with rifle ready. At the horses' heads a stooped, rawboned man with leathery features, sharp nose, countenance curiously worried and intent, who bleated a curt demand in Spanish.

"Where going?"

His voice was flat. A harsh croak; the voice of the deaf.

"To Gonzales," Durant answered in English. He heard the girl catch her breath, heard her echo the word in whisper of astonishment, as her eyes went to him. "Gonzales!"

"Where from?" snapped the man afoot, who wore moccasins.

"Bejar."

"What say?"

"He says Bejar, Smith!" This was one of the horsemen, a man of fiery red hair under wide hat, sunburned, shrewd and jovial face, and keen eyes.

"Hey!" Smith spoke up quickly, his round blue eyes on Durant's lips. "El Alamo! What about it?"

Durant looked into the blue eyes, stark and merciless.

"All dead; the Alamo is taken."

"What say?" Hand went up behind ear. Red-hair intervened again, excitedly.

"He says the Alamo's took, Deef! Dead—hey, dammit! What kind o' lie is this?"

Durant looked at the speaker, his own visage calm, unhurried, Indianlike in its patience.

"No lie, my friends. Not a man remains alive."

Doña Amadora noted the staring eyes, the thin snarls, and turned in terror.

"What is it, Vicente?"

"I've told them that the Alamo garrison are all dead."

"It is so, *señores!*" she burst out, careless whether the Texans understood her Spanish—though they did. "They are dead, every one. It was by General Santa Anna's orders. We have nothing to do with it. Don Vicente is not among the troops who were there—I swear it, and may the Virgin hear me! You must let us pass—"

The sharp nose of Deef Smith twitched about his snarling lips.

"Plain English was enough, I reckon," he croaked tersely, and stepped back. His rifle came to the cock. "Off, damn you! Understand me?"

"Hold on, Deef!" It was the redhead again. "What are you up to now?"

"Kill him," snapped Deef Smith, blue eyes narrowed upon Durant.

"You can't do that, you old 'Pache!"

"Hell I can't! You heard what he said. Mexican sojer, ain't he? Scalp him."

The second horseman pressed in.

"No, Deef, no! Karnes and I say no. We'll have to take 'em both to Gonzales. Hold 'em there for Houston and let him decide."

Smith, hand behind ear, nodded balefully. He was a man of few words. Then Durant interposed, calmly.

"I'm no Mexican, my friends, but an American. I was with Fannin, took a message from him to Travis at Bejar, got there too late, and was jailed. This lady helped me escape—as did the uniform. As it happens, you don't have to take us to Gonzales; we're going there."

THE RED-HEADED Karnes squinted contemptuously at him, and spat.

"Happens is good. Happens you're in Mexican uniform; that's wuss. Happens you speak two tongues, but happens my name's Karnes, and yonder's Deef Smith, the best scout on the border! What do you call yourself?"

"Durant. Gordon Durant, of Tennessee."

"The hell you say!" Karnes leaned over and shouted at the scout. "Says his name's Durant, Tennessee! Ever hear tell of that name in these parts?"

"Nope—hey! Mebbe I did." Deef Smith glowered. "Blackleg rascal who turned Mex, wan't that it? I disremember. Better kill him right here."

"Not yet, confound you! Wait till we learn more. We'll turn back." Karnes gave Durant a hard, direct look. "Maybe you're lying! I hate to believe you. Word has spread of some feller with a name like yours in the Mex army, murdering settlers and looting. If you're him, you'll hang quick. You and your woman come along with us."

Deef Smith's eyes were as sharp as his nose. He gestured with his rifle.

"Suthin' behind his saddle. Plunder. Take a look."

"No time now," Karnes returned. "Leave it for the gin'ral."

Mumbling, Deef Smith went to retrieve his horse. Doña Amadora's white face turned to Durant again.

"And now, Vicente?"

"To Gonzales with them. You're safe; your leather case is safe. They don't steal from women. All your difficulties are ended, so be at ease."

She glanced doubtfully at the watching men, at the brown, inflexible features of Durant, hard as those of an Indian.

"But you, Vicente? What of you?"

Knowing that these others probably understood Spanish, Durant smiled slightly.

"Perfectly safe, *doña*. I've only to see General Houston, and all's well,"

A grunt from Karnes, a word from the returned Deef Smith, and the party took the road. Durant in the lead, with Karnes and Handy, as the third man was named. Deef Smith following with Doña Amadora. Small use for her to talk with him; he had no eye for woman's wiles.

The two in front spoke little, asked nothing at first. That news from the Alamo had shocked them into silence. After a time, a question or two. Durant responded curtly. He was of no mind to explain, appeal, insist. Beneath his shirt was that which would resolve all doubts in the right quarter. Meantime, the uniform he wore was damning. And there was that mention of Vincent Durant, or Durante as he carried it among the Mexicans. Murdering settlers and looting, eh? That was to be expected.

"All dead. No prisoners."

Those words were enough. An occasional oath, a mention of some name, some friend; the three scouts spoke little else. A taciturn journey. They met no one on the road.

So passed the day, and with gathering evening grew Gonzales, on the east bank of the Guadalupe river. A few lights were twinkling from the houses of the town, and campfires from a small encampment of troops, when the horses splashed across the ford. Deef Smith barked inquiry at sentinels on the camp outskirts.

"Cap here yet?"

"The gin'ral? Yep; come in 'bout four this evening. Over in that tent yonder. What you got, Deef?"

"Couple Mex. For Cap."

"Any news from Bejar?"

"Mebbe." The reply was terse and grim, as usual.

T H E T E N T flaps were open to the night; the interior was lighted only by the fire in front of the opening. The busy flames flickered upon the figures of two men, both booted, spurred and belted. One was seated on an upturned stump, the other upon an empty whisky keg, methodically whittling a pine stick with a clasp-knife.

It was this latter who took Durant's eye, not so much by the buckskin jacket and vest of Cherokee cut and devices, or by the wool hat at his feet with brave feather in the crown, as by the powerful form and leonine visage. Durant recognized it instantly. A massive man, scraggly bearded, thick chestnut hair, tanned but fair skin, with deeply challenging blue eyes under a commanding brow. A noble countenance, strongly characterized, wilful, impulsive, but self-contained.

Deef Smith slipped from the saddle, rifle in hand, and strode into the tent.

"Fetched a party for you, Cap."

"Bring them in."

Durant stiffly dismounted and helped the girl down. Smith, vigilant, nodded them inside. The man on the keg rose with an exclamation and gallant gesture. He was tall, well over six feet.

"What's this? A lady?"

"She may have my stump, general." Major Hockley, his aide, arose. Doña Amadora, interpreting his word and gesture, accepted the stump and sank down upon it, gathering her cloak around her knees.

"Ketched 'em on Bejar road this mornin'," said Deef Smith. "Karnes, Handy and me."

"From Bejar?" The voice was full chested, resonant, and Deef had no difficulty in hearing it.

"He says so. Claims to be an American. Damned renegade. Better let me kill him."

Houston looked at Durant, his blue eyes icy cold. The half smile on Durant's lips intensified their anger. They held no recognition. How should they, across the years?

"You're a Mexican officer, sir?"

"I am not, sir," Durant replied. "I am Gordon Durant, of Tennessee."

Houston's shaggy brows drew down. The name struck echoes, evidently.

"You speak my tongue, but your uniform speaks more plainly, sir. You seem to befoul a good name and the name of my State. You are from San Antonio de Bejar? What news of the battle there?"

"Ended." Durant spoke laconically. "Every man in the Alamo killed."

"What?" Houston's leonine head jerked back as though he had received a blow in the face. He blindly sought for the keg and sank down upon it.

"Likely a damned lie, Cap," blurted Deef Smith. Houston shook his head and turned to his companion.

"You heard, Hockley? As we feared. On our way here from the convention, we listened in vain for the signal gun from Travis. It failed the day we started, the sixth. Good God! Why didn't they retire when ordered? Why didn't they receive aid—from Fannin, from the force there, from the council?" He turned to Durant. "This happened when?"

"On the sixth, sir. The ashes are cold."

"The ashes?"

"The bodies were burned by Santa Anna as a gesture of contempt—"

"My God!" Houston started up. "And you—you were there? You, in the uniform of murderers, dare to stand here and inform me—"

"Certainly." Durant regarded the icy blue gaze with cold calm. "Why not? I've nothing to fear from you. In fact, I have other information which may be important."

HOUSTON PASSED a hand over his eyes and resumed his seat. Deef Smith, who had darted outside, now reappeared. He was bearing the leather casket.

"Suthin' else, Cap. Tied up in a poncho; right hefty. Mebbe loot."

"The private property of this lady, General Houston," put in Durant. His impassive mien, his steady, controlled voice, his curt, unexplained words, had gradually focused him into the dominant figure in the tent. "Her private valuables are here, I believe."

"Oh! The lady, yes," murmured Houston, with a glance at the *doña*. "Her name?"

"Doña Amadora de la Vega. I escorted her and her property to safety here."

There was interruption; Houston turned his head with a change of attention. Sounds came from without. Shrieks of women, shouts and a rising tide of wrath in men's voices. The general spoke quickly.

"The news has broken out among the families and friends of those men—Smith! Find Karnes and Handy. Spread word that I say the report from Bejar is false. We'll have panic on our hands if we don't check it. Tell everyone that Sam Houston says the report is false. Jump!"

Deef Smith nodded and went out at the run, noiseless in his moccasins. Houston looked at his aide.

"Hockley, any panic among the settlers will ruin us. We must have calm resolution above all else. Later tonight, spread the news that the report is confirmed; by that time we'll have the situation under control—what's this, now?"

New interruption. Again Houston came to his feet, this time in politeness. The cold poise of Durant was abruptly shattered. His eyes widened. A tide of passionate dark color flooded into his cheeks; he tensed as he stood, watching the newcomer.

A young woman, this, panting, who ran in past the fire and halted, with eyes only for Houston. Pink calico dress, blue eyes dilated, flaxen hair loosened by her exertions.

"General! Is it true?" she burst forth. "They say that the

Alamo has fallen and that Santa Anna and his whole army are marching on Gonzales—"

"A wild rumor, my dear Miss Hittel," Houston broke in. "No, no, don't believe these infernal tales! I've sent men out to learn the truth. Later tonight I'll know it. Until then, give your help in getting the other settlers calmed."

Doña Amadora stirred, turned, spoke in soft contralto.

"Vicente! Who is this *señorita*, Vicente? What is it all about?"

"It is nothing," said Durant to her.

The interruption had drawn the attention of Faith Hittel. Her gaze swept to Durant and settled there, incredulous, horrified. The look in her eyes broke his reserve.

"Faith!" he exclaimed. "Surely—"

Her blue eyes struck frostily at Doña Amadora, back at him. She shrank a little, half in anger, half in disdain and contempt.

"You!" she cried, "You again—oh!"

"You know this man?" Houston asked quickly.

"I do not!" she replied. "Rather, I know him only to loathe him. I must go. Thank you, general, for your kindness—"

"One moment," intervened Houston. "You know this Spanish lady?"

"Assuredly not," was her scornful reply.

"Patience, my dear, patience!" The towering, haggard man could be gentle, as he proved. "You and your father—I have met you both. I know your house. You can help me, if you will. This Spanish lady has traveled far and is worn out; she needs the attention of a woman, and secure shelter. This camp of men is no place for her. You understand? May I ask your help?"

FAITH HITTEL paused in obvious reluctance, then replied:

"I suppose so. As you know, my father and I are alone since my mother's death. We could not deny your appeal, and her need."

"Thank you, my dear!" Houston took her hand, patted it, and

smiled. "Spoken like the heart of gold you are. This chest belongs to the lady. Major Hockley, will you be good enough to carry it and escort the two ladies?"

Conscious that this conversation regarded her, Doña Amadora was gazing bewildered. Durant turned and addressed her.

"*Doña*, you are to be sheltered in the house of this *señorita*, for the night. The officer yonder will take your casket; your jewels are perfectly safe."

"Thanks to the saints!" She rose. "I am wearied to death. But you, Vicente? You are not coming? You know this *señorita?*"

No time for the truth now. Get rid of her at all costs, settle matters with Sam Houston, arrange his own affair.

"I'll see you in the morning," he said. "I must remain and talk with the general. All is well, so fear not."

"But I do not understand. *Madre de Dios!*" she faltered. "Why does this girl seem so scornful of us? We've done no harm. Well, no matter; until tomorrow, my Vicente!"

So, with a troubled parting gaze, she turned and joined the girl waiting at the threshold of the tent. Major Hockley picked up the chest.

"When you've seen the ladies safe, Hockley," said Houston, "kindly find Captain Desauque. I want him here immediately. Good night, ladies!"

So they were gone. Houston swung around, resumed his seat, and gestured Durant to the stump opposite. His gaze was piercing.

"Sit down, sir; there's much here I fail to understand. How long were you in San Antonio and when?"

Durant considered. "About fifteen hours. Yesterday."

"You're damned curt. You're attached to Santa Anna's forces?"

"No. I'm an American—"

"That proves nothing. There are dozens of Americans in the

Mexican army, scores of them. Smith declares you're a renegade. Why were you in Bejar?"

"Two reasons. To find and kill a man, and to deliver a message. On the way, I acquired this uniform and a horse, to serve my purpose. The message was from Colonel Fannin to Colonel Travis—"

"What? Fannin?" Houston caught at the name. "He knows you?"

"Of course." Durant knew with whom he dealt. This man, who had lived half his life among the Indians, could best be reached by such laconic speech. There was recognition to come in its time. "I arrived too late with his message."

"Too late," murmured Houston, and struck fist on knee. "It should not have been—before my God, I say it should not have been!" A gigantic emotion convulsed his rugged, worn features; then he had himself in hand. "Goliad! There, were you? Then what is Colonel Fannin's muster?"

"Upwards of four hundred men, sir, chiefly parties of volunteers from the United States. The Mobile Grays, the Georgia Volunteers, the Kentucky Mustangs, the Huntsville Volunteers from Tennessee, and so forth. A detachment of Texas artillery. A company of mounted men, sent to Matagorda."

"Correct. If I only knew what Urrea was doing—"

"I can tell you that. The man from whom I took this uniform carried dispatches. They were from Urrea. He has taken San Patricio, destroyed Colonel Grant's command to the last man, and was about to advance on Goliad."

"Those dispatches? Where are they?"

"I was caught at San Antonio and had to act as the bearer. I delivered them to Santa Anna."

"What!" Houston straightened back in an access of sudden fury. "You call yourself an American, sir—you admit that you stood before that hellhound and did not kill him?"

DURANT GRIMLY smiled. "I postponed the pleasure,

Mr. Houston, as I suggest that you postpone the flights of oratory. Besides, I had my own errand there in Bejar. Unhappily, I was placed under arrest—I am still ignorant of the reason—"

"Your private errand, yes; I remember. To kill a man." Houston took no offense, but his brows drew down. "Somewhere I have seen you before, sir. But what was this errand? The name of the man you desired to kill?"

"My half-brother, Vincent Durant. In New Orleans, under cover of darkness, he took my name and assumed my identity, with intent to ruin the girl to whom I was engaged."

The stark, simple words shocked Houston out of his slouch.

"And did he succeed, sir?"

"No."

"By God, sir, you should kill the scoundrel!" exclaimed Houston. "Your half-brother, you say? Why, the thing is incredible! You have married the lady?"

"No. Vincent had forged my father's name for ten thousand dollars and fled from Tennessee, leaving my father to die in poverty. Colonel Davy Crockett wrote me that he had seen the rascal in Nacogdoches. I trailed him to New Orleans and lost him there, after the incident which I have mentioned. He entered the Mexican service. I followed him to Mexico, trailed him south and then north again to Texas."

Houston was interested. "But, sir, the lady! She is informed of the deception?"

"She and her father were in New Orleans, on the way to take up land in Texas. I had no chance to see her; I could only write her, informing her of the truth."

"Where is she now, then?"

"You have seen her. She is Faith Hittel, who was just now here."

"What!" Houston stared at him. "But she saw you, you addressed her, and she scorned you!"

"Certainly. You heard me addressed by Doña Amadora.

Naturally, Faith thought me to be Vincent, since we closely resemble each other. So Santa Anna thought me to be Vincent—"

Houston started, and his face darkened.

"And by the Eternal, so do I!" he broke in. "This is a specious tale, but that Spanish lady bears witness against you. Durant? You cloak yourself in a name you do not deserve. It rings in my recollection as a good name. The Spanish lady knows you—"

Durant smiled. The moment had come.

"Vincent had cozened her into loving him. He was to flee from Bejar with her and her jewels. She took me for him—and I saved her person and her property by bringing her here. Your scouts met us. As for the name of Durant, sir, you should recollect it."

"Yes?" Houston frowned uncertainly. "How so?"

"At the Horseshoe Bend battle with the Creeks, in 1814, you received an arrow in the thigh. You ordered a fellow officer to pull it out; and under threat of your upraised sword, he did so."

Houston became intent. "What you say is common knowledge, sir."

"That man was my father," Durant pursued. "After he left the service, he kept that blood-stained arrowhead. My father had two sons; I was the child of his first marriage. My half-brother Vincent bears a strong likeness to me, but I admit no kinship. He has ever hated me. To pass himself off for me has ever been his damnable delight."

"By the Eternal, I remember you now!" blared Houston, then suddenly checked himself and sank back on his keg. "Or do I?" he asked craftily. Durant smiled.

"You should, sir. When you were governor of Tennessee my father sent me to you with a letter from him, asking that you recommend me for an army commission; I took the arrowhead with me as a reminder of him. Let me tell you, sir, how I found you. I was shown in to where you stood, clad in a red calico Indian shirt and shaving with your hunting knife."

HOUSTON'S DEEP blue eyes were no longer icy, but warm, full, resplendent. He nodded slightly, and prompted:

"Well, sir? And then—"

"Then you bade me keep that arrowhead as token that a soldier must be willing to suffer for his country. You presented me with the knife and its Cherokee beaded sheath. Later, I had the arrowpoint set into the wooden haft of the knife. Here it is."

He produced the knife from beneath his shirt, slipped the thong, and handed the weapon to Houston. A large, ordinary, heavy knife with razor edge, and set into the haft a barbed iron arrowhead, dark with rust. Houston seized upon it, his eyes glinting on the beaded sheath with softened memories.

"The same, the same," he murmured. "The sheath, the knife, the very point!" His fixed gaze, intent and penetrating as that of an eagle, lifted to Durant's face. "And the story. The evidence is complete. Your face, sir, speaks more eloquently than you are aware. I bid you welcome. The lady who scorned you shall know the truth. I myself will tell her, and she herself will welcome you on your return."

"On my return!" Durant echoed. Houston smiled suddenly. In some respects these two men were extremely alike—in their almost Indian reserve and reticence, their cold inward poise, their sudden abrupt utterance.

"Precisely." Houston relaxed, extended the sheathed knife again to Durant, and drew a deep breath. Their personal affairs were ended, the subject was closed. "I'm sending Captain De-sauque at once to Colonel Fannin with orders to destroy his fortifications, bury his artillery, and retire to Victoria on the Guadalupe. We shall have to unite on a line of defense, lest he be cut off at Goliad. I have short of four hundred men, with less than two days' rations, poorly armed and clothed. We must abandon Gonzales and also retire to Victoria. If we can avert a panic on the frontier, we can join a respectable force armed with vengeance upon the invaders of the republic. I'm sending

Deef Smith to scout toward San Antonio again, to pick up news. And you—you speak Spanish well, I perceive."

"Well enough," Durant rejoined.

"Precisely. Then you can—ah, here's Hockley with Desauque. Come in, Captain! Major Hockley, will you take down a dispatch to Colonel Fannin?"

A sudden bursting energy welled up and broke forth in the man, scattered his weariness. He dictated a curt dispatch to Fannin. Hockley, squatting on his hams, wrote to the dictation. Captain Desauque, an upstanding, soldierly man, waited impassively until the letter was signed and sealed, then thrust it away.

"Captain, you'll leave instantly. Make all speed to Goliad."

"Yes, sir."

"Look upon this man." Towering, Houston laid a hand on Durant's shoulder. "Look upon the man, not the garments. He has my confidence. I vouch for him. I desire the fact to be made known."

Desauque keenly gazed, and flashed a smile; then, with a salute, strode away. Houston resumed his seat and nodded to Durant.

"I WANT you to go to General Urrea—that is, if you'll volunteer for the job. You know what it means. You're in uniform; you can represent yourself as from General Santa Anna with orders that Urrea shall remain where he is and not advance on Goliad. Say you've lost or destroyed your dispatches, any damned thing you like. You have wit, sir. You can hoodwink that rascal and gain us time. Time! I need time to rally the Texan army, to procure powder and provisions, to retreat and join forces. Fannin's four hundred men, well trained, well drilled, may mean life or death to Texas. I'll give you credentials, in case you meet any of our own scouts. Durant, will you undertake this job?"

"Gladly, sir. But there are complications. This uniform was identified by General Filisola and others; the man from whom I took it was a member of Urrea's staff. My face—rather, that

of my half-brother Vincent—might not be known at San Patricio, but this uniform certainly would."

Hockley nodded assent to this. "The cap and the facing where
the tunic is parted indicate the Tampico Battalion, general. And
the Tampico Dragoons are with Urrea."

"Very well." Houston's brows drew down. "We'll drum up
another garb for you, Durant. Get some sleep, then be off. I'll
see to a horse—but you have one, eh?"

"Yes. I'm confident that I can handle the matter, so far as
Urrea is concerned," replied Durant. "What about Doña
Amadora?"

"The Spanish lady? Fear not; at the first opportunity, I'll have
her sent where she desires, with her valuables. Now, what about
a bite to eat with us? I've only some dried beef; we must all
make the best of it. As for bed, there are some blankets in the
corner. Help yourself to them."

Later, Durant stretched out, rolled in a blanket, his brain
weighing the odds of this venture ahead. When he faced Urrea,
what would he find? Suspicion, recognition, accusation? Probably not; Santa Anna would not have acted quickly. Perhaps
Vincent lay trapped in Bejar, having taken his place. And Faith
was near! Her name sang through his thoughts. She was near,
she would know the truth from Houston, all would be well
again!

And all the while, there on the stump before the dying fire,
that huge form bowed over clasp knife and pine stick, while
the shavings gathered. Upon the solitude of the tent crept occasional rumbled murmurs from a soul now despairing, now
indomitable, altogether heroic.

"A panic—men in arms fleeing to join their families—retreat,
retreat! No men, no powder. Ground of my own choosing—we
can whip them one to ten. They'll blame me, but I'll bend them
to the vision I see—oh, Travis, Travis! Where are you, Davy
Crockett! Where are you, Bowie!"

And the leonine head bowed, with a glitter of tears on the shaggy cheeks.

CHAPTER V

BROTHER MEETS BROTHER

THREE HOURS of sleep, no more; then Durant was off.

Little Gonzales had been hushed of its panic, for the moment. Fires had dwindled to dulling embers. The tiny Texan muster, camped here in the end of the Guadalupe, slept, while a wild morrow gathered way like a storming freshet. Within brief time, fire and sword were to sweep town and farms away in wild rout of destruction.

The murder-accursed uniform was gone now. Durant wore rough country costume, had pistols at his saddle, and in his pocket a paper. "Gonzales, March 11, 1836. To Whom It May Concern: The bearer, Gordon Durant, etc., etc." And signed by "Sam Houston, Commander In Chief, Texas Army." Houston himself had wakened Durant and sped him on his way.

Even then there had been mist in the air and the stars were thin.

Now, hours later, it was impossible to tell how near was the dawn. The fog had come rolling over the prairie from the south. Gonzales was leagues behind; Victoria, in the southwest beyond Goliad, was still across a no-man's land of treacherous friendship and open hostility. Once Durant struck the traveled road from Bejar to the south, he would have his bearings and could make good time.

Here in the sea of desert fog and chaparral he had no bearings. The horse ambled aimlessly, without choice of direction when the bridle reins were taxed, and finally came to a halt. With a shrug, Durant swung off, to curb impatience and await the thinning of the fog before the advance of daylight.

Vast smothering silence weighted the air. Sitting with the reins of his drooping animal over his arm, Durant dozed. He waked, finally, to realization that the gray of the night had whitened. The form of his horse, wet and motionless, was distinct amid the drifting wraiths of fog-fleece. Birds twittered, and overhead grew the lightening sky.

Durant thoughtfully freshened the priming of his pistols and climbed into the saddle. He tightened rein and legs; the horse moved stiffly forward. Sharpened instincts helped to set the course. Where the fog thinned, diffused light from greater brightness indicated the east. By the warmth that began to flood him like a soft breath, he could know the sun had risen.

The fog still clung to the ground, however. Save for the scuff of hooves, the creak of saddle leather, the scrape and crackle of twigs in the brush, all sounds were swaddled in the dampness.

Gradually, the fog broke. Sun and morning breeze swept it from higher levels; it lingered in the bottoms, so that in the vast sea one rode now upon a clear crest, now in the next trough. In one of these troughs, a long shallow draw spotted with brush, the horse struck into a trail. Here the fog had thinned, but the draw was eerie with eddying wisps of mist and the ghostly shapes of taller shrubs.

The trail led to water, perhaps. The horse pricked ears and snorted—whether in alarm, in query, in recognition, was hard to say. Then, at a turn of the crooked trail hoof-prints had swerved aside into the fringing covert of green. Durant reined short to examine them, for they were fresh. With head bared, he leaned over, estimating and peering. Then he straightened up again, trying to pierce the fog-eddies.

A rustle of something breaking the brush—a stone flung, perchance. As he turned toward the sound, from the opposite direction came a swish in the air. A lash flicked about his throat, jerked taut. Durant was plucked violently from the saddle. A blinding flash athwart his brain as he fell—it was the end of everything.

FROM LIFE to death, from death back to life. So the thought flitted through his mind as his eyes heavily opened to sunlight. His gaze wandered, then slowly cleared. Memory returned. He was lying on his back, head slightly bolstered up. And there in front of him was—himself!

Himself indeed, no idle fancy. His sight, his brain, focused at once. Vincent squatted there regarding him; Vincent, wearing his garments, smiling sardonically and flipping away a cigarette.

"Awake, brother?" came the taunting words. "And how are you this morning?"

The resemblance was striking enough. No twin, Vincent yet had forthright, hard features of the same pattern, readily adapted for tricks of expression calculated to deceive acquaintance or stranger alike. Stature matched closely enough, the voice was that of Gordon Durant itself; thus the devil lurked behind the cross.

The two horses stood close at hand. Gordon Durant realized now that he was stripped of outer garments and securely trussed; ankles bound together with rawhide, and wrists fastened behind his back. His head, he conceived, was pillowed upon a roll— probably jacket and trousers belonging to Vincent, who now wore his.

"You damned scoundrel!" he rasped. His throat was sore and swollen, his muscles stiff. Vincent grinned.

"Be civil, brother, be civil! Anyway, you've got a tongue again. So use it. Where are Doña Amadora and her chest—particularly her chest?"

"Go to hell," snarled Durant. He writhed to free himself, only to sink back in exhaustion. The rawhide thongs had been well laid.

"Don't waste your breath, good brother; you need it all. You've

"Off, damn you!
Understand me?"

had a bad fall, I believe. Come, tell me where you left our pretty Amadora and that tight little packet of hers?"

"She and her property are safe from you," said Durant. His voice, his eyes, told his unuttered curses. "You'll not find her through me. Up to more of your deviltry, eh?"

Vincent laughed softly.

"How we love each other! But all the same, I think I will find her—and through you, also." He watched Durant for a long time, a murky devil leaping in his dark gaze. "It will be in Gonzales; you've just come from there. Yes, I'll betake myself to Gonzales. You approve? Disapprove?"

"I approve of whatever will get you killed like the mad dog you are."

"You'd like to do it yourself, eh?" Vincent chuckled. "Gonzales; the paper you carried tells me you've come from there. Thanks for the loan of your clothes, brother. And that precious knife of yours; no, I wouldn't dare leave you with a knife. I know the story of this one, and perhaps Houston would like to be reminded of it."

"You'll not dare face Houston," snapped Durant.

"I may not have to, brother. But the knife is comforting; so is the paper, of course. And my stay there will be short. Santa Anna has sent two thousand troops that way, so I'll not linger. As soon as I've found the little Amadora and her leather casket—and Faith! Yes, I hear that our Faith is there at Gonzales. My friends bring me news, you see—you like the idea, eh?"

He laughed in delight at the raging curses of the bound man.

"You devil! What makes you think she's there?" cried Durant, presently.

"I know it very well; she and that fool of a miserly rascal, her father," said Vincent coolly. "This time she'll be fonder of me than she was before—eh?" He leaned forward, his smile died, a dark flush of savage passion invaded his features. "But I mean to have that casket. Do you think I'll let ten thousand dollars in gold slip out of my hands without a play for the money? Not much!"

DURANT WAS startled, immobile, staring. "Ten thousand dollars? Don't be a fool. Why, she said—"

He broke off, as Vincent nodded placidly.

"Don't get excited; the money's not for you. Yes, she probably said—and thought—the casket held her jewels. Well, no longer! They went to the monte bank. I preferred the gold, and had only to substitute. An easy matter, when a *caballero* is loved by a confiding doncella. But I had to get the gold out of Bejar, you see."

"You seem to specialize in that amount," Durant sneered. Suddenly he remembered Jacopo and the demands of El Tuerto. And this rat had to get the gold out of Bejar! Then this might explain his arrest—might explain everything! "Stolen gold, I suppose?"

"We don't call it that in official circles," Vincent said easily. "A game of catch as catch can. First to His Excellency for his war levy; then to me, Captain Vicente Durante, for my services as a Mexican officer. I hear you got to Bejar ahead of me, eh? But here I am; all roads lead to this trail."

"So, renegade! I suppose you're one of the victors of the Alamo?" and Durant spat in cold fury. Vincent shook his head.

"My genius was better suited to the quartermaster department. Result, five hundred golden *onzas*, five hundred double eagles! Santa Anna can get more; but he's damnably stingy. He begrudged me the trifle, so I had to take it myself. Our little Amadora and her jewels made opportunity. Clever, eh?"

Explanation here, and no mistake. Explanation of all; no wonder they had been so astonished to see the deserter, the embezzler, suddenly appear with dispatches!

"You'll need to be clever," Durant said. "Don't forget El Tuerto."

Then, at last, Vincent blanched a trifle, started, narrowed his black eyes.

"You know, eh? You must have met with the sign; they took you for me! I see. Well, no need to remind me, brother; that's one of the debts I don't pay."

So saying, he came to his feet, and a snarl twisted his lips.

"I'm paying my score against you, though. Damn you, Gordon, I've always hated you! I dare say you came into Bejar to kill me, eh? And you nearly did it. A sweet mess I found there! A *ranchero*, one Pedro Ortiz, thought he recognized me by sight. The fool nabbed me and was for making a scene, accused high and low—treachery, lies, murder! It seems I had promised to take him to Santa Anna. Well, I took him, into a back room I know about," and Vincent's snarl changed to a laugh. "He won't talk now, at least! You can thank me for having friends, brother. Else you'd die with your face to the wall instead of to the sky! Well, I picked up what had happened, ran into my friends—and there was the devil to explain, thanks to you! I had to take a slope and try getting track of Amadora and casket before she opened it. I knew you wouldn't go to Cuba; neither would I. New Orleans is far enough, eh?"

"For you and the *doña?*" asked Durant.

"For me and the chest, brother," was the complacent response. "And while I was waiting out the fog in the bush, who should come riding along but you! So I tossed my lasso around your neck, and here you are."

"And now what?" Durant uttered. "Murder, I suppose?"

"I don't know why I didn't break your neck, or keep the noose tight!" Vincent paced back and forth, frowning. "I could guess enough, by what I found on you. Maybe I wanted to see your eyes when they looked on me. And yet I shrink a little from putting a knife into you—can you believe it?"

"Not I," said Durant. "You ruined our father and killed him. You've played the devil a score of times. And mark me, I'll some day kill you myself!"

Vincent nodded. "So you think. Yet—well, it's strange enough! Now that I could do it, my hand holds back; not from love of you, comprehend! Bad luck in it, perhaps."

H E   W E N T   to the horses and suddenly swung up into Durant's saddle. "Good horse, good pistols," he said, and laughed. "Well—I am you, brother! Once more. And I may have you shot as a spy yet. But you'll rot before that rawhide rots, so farewell. I leave you with the buzzards. And yet—"

He hesitated, his eyes lingering on the prostrate figure. His hand went out to one of the pistols. Then, with a quick flirt of his shoulders, he squared around and drove in spurs, and went cantering away, leading his own horse after.

Gordon Durant lay passive, consumed by hatred, wrung by emotion, for a space. Then, falling calm, he looked down at his ankles, considered them attentively. The rawhide there was bright and flexible.

The morning had warmed apace. The thinned fog wandered in vagrant clouds, dismayed spectres of the night vainly seeking sanctuary from the devouring sun. The sun would presently be triumphant over earth as he already was in the sky. The drying rawhide would tauten and shrink.

Durant stirred, drew breath of resolution. He bridged himself by shoulders and heels, striving to force his joined wrists down past his hips. If once he could slide between his two arms and bring his wrists in front, he could use his teeth like a trap-pinched animal.

Not so easily done. He sat up, wrestling again with himself. But although he strained till the joints cracked, he could not get those coupled wrists past the hips. He was too long in the body for that feat. Too long of leg, too short of body, he found, for bending double and applying teeth to ankle bonds. Beaded with clammy sweat, panting, he desisted. Sweat! If he could only drench himself with sweat! At that, he was racing the sun's heat.

He sat up, bent over, shoulders strained, and gazed desperately around. Behind him lay cotton blouse and pantaloons. Vincent's cast-off shapeless brogans gaped to the air, at one side. Where was the trail he had followed? Impossible to find. The brush had closed it out of sight.

Here was another trail, however, made by the rope dragging a lax body—his own. Durant smiled, with a catch of breath. He set his lips, rose to his knees, then came to his feet. He went hopping, stumbling, falling, crawling on his knees only to buck-jump again until tripped off balance, along that back trail blazed by the weighted rope.

An interminable way of slow effort; but at last it ended. There was the trail, the spot where he had been noosed; here the hoofprints of his standing horse. Did the trail lead to water, as he had conceived? Painfully, he bucked his way along it, praying to the capricious gods of chance that courage be rewarded; that the trail led, in thankful time, to moisture.

He gathered himself for continued effort; fell and rose again, gaining painful footage by dint of wearied muscle and straining nerves, holding his bruised body to the task grimly. The trail did end, to his glaring, distended eyes. It broadened and blunted at a patch of coarse seepage grass still low-bent with dew and fog, green with moisture from succulent roots at water's edge.

With a harsh, hoarse cry and one final desperate lunge, Durant flung himself into the pool. Not to bury his flaming face, but to wallow upon his back, burying his fire-tortured wrists deep and ever deeper, until they were enveloped in coal mud. The grasses showered his face with wetness as he turned his head from side to side. With this, and with his happy wrists, he knew content, and rested.

TIME MARCHED with the mounting sun. His energy was refreshed, his muscles were renewed. The movements of his wrists became freer as the soaked rawhide began to yield and stretch. To the constant strain of his wrists the tether lengthened. After all, he needed but little play. Presently he sat up again and clenched his teeth for the grand effort.

He writhed and twisted. Motes danced before his surcharged eyes. His arms almost tore from their sockets, the skin seemed to be rasped from his sodden hips; then, suddenly, he was through the loop of flesh. A gasp of relief escaped him. The joined wrists were forward under his knees. He doubled with knees sharply flexed, with feet drawn in. Still he failed, and tried again in frantic desperation. By sheer force of will, exerted until bone and sinew and compressed lungs were racked with torment, he got his wrists under his two heels.

Now he was fast in a ball. Again—again, until the world turned red! His wrists inched along, slipped thankfully. Then he passed them over his toes and fell back to uncoil, to straighten out and lie panting, relaxed.

Only for a moment. He sat up and put his teeth to the bonds. He gnawed at the thong until his gums bled, until the frayed, slippery hide came apart and shredded between his jaws. Parted!

With savage teeth he unlaced the wrappings. Thank God! A man animal with hands for use; to be no more than that was enough. His hands were free.

Oh, for his knife again, or even a saw-edged pebble! He picked and pecked at the ankle bonds with fingers and nails, with bits of stick. Nails broke, sticks slid from the wet rawhide, but the knots loosened. Loosened, and came free. It was done.

The impossible lay behind him. Durant stood up—torn, scratched, drenched with wet and mud—gauntly free for vengeance, like a ragged Monte Cristo emerged from dungeon, sack and depths. His wrists bled, his face was savage with violent exertion and more violent thoughts. He set off, back along the little trail. A man who must travel the thorny prairie afoot needs covering for soles and body.

To this end, Vincent had been obliging. Grimly, Durant slid into the shabby garments, the shapeless leather.

The sun was high in the clear blue sky. The fog had vanished. Durant trudged on at best speed. He required no trail, but hastened regardless. Gonzales! If he might overtake Vincent there, he had the rat! Durant could see nothing beyond this, and did not cast further. Nose to trail, knife to hand! Houston was no fool, to be gulled by that scoundrel after hearing the truth.

Thus Durant had footed for an hour or more, when he heard the nicker of a horse as in salutation. It came from a clump of green in a hollow, over to his right. He halted, then turned for it. A horse! Perhaps another dragoon officer to topple into death—what matter? He was a man with rage in his heart, a grip in his ten fingers and no fear in his heels. He headed for the clump, straight as a wolf swerving to the scent. Perhaps Vincent, or Vincent's offcast horse?

But no. Carefully he broke through the mask of greenery and peered ahead. A single horse, saddled, head hanging low; and beside the animal an outstretched figure, couched, wrapped in cloak, pillowed head adrift with lustrous hair—Doña Amadora!

The *doña*, and alone. Incredulous, Durant stared, squirmed through the greenery, stood looking about uncertainly. As he stood, the girl opened her eyes upon him. She stared, unbelieving; then she sat up suddenly, stared again, uttered a glad cry.

"Vicente! You! God be praised—you've escaped and have found me here! But this is a miracle!"

DURANT GRIMACED; Doña Amadora be damned! But her bivouac promised values other than the lady herself. Ten thousand dollars! Spoil of the enemy, and a rightful heritage to him besides. He noted the pillow that upheld her head—it was the poncho wrapped about the casket. Yet, how on earth had she come here, and why?

"What does it mean?" he demanded. "What brought you here?"

If he showed none of the gladness she expected, at least she paid little heed to his stiff aloofness.

"I could not let you know, *querido mio*," she babbled. She was beautiful, she was capable, she was enough to fire any eye; but the black eyes of Durant fired not. "It was the old man of the house where I was staying."

"Who? Hittel?" snapped Durant. "What did he do?"

"Sent me away." She was wide-eyed, eager, lovely and joyous with the flush of sleep. "I do not think the *señorita* knew. She did not like me or you, remember; but this was the old man. He woke me very early, long before dawn. He beckoned me outside and carried my chest, here. The horse was ready, I was to ride away; he said men were coming to rob me. It was for me to leave at once, in the fog and the night. May God reward him for his kindness!"

"May the devil pay him!" growled Durant harshly. "What was that old hellion up to? All a cursed lie. You were under Houston's protection."

She stared. "But he warned me! He was very honest, Vicente.

Here is the casket, to prove it. But I have been afraid for you!
I knew those men were angry with you, Vicente, and would
have killed you. And you escaped? I can see for myself. You
found other clothes and got away. *Viva!* But you're afoot, you've
had a hard time—my poor Vicente!"

She was all compassion. Durant scowled in thought. What
was old Hittel's game? He knew the man; greedy, a miser of
unscrupulous clutch, and bitter shrewd withal.

"You're hurt?" The *doña* came to her feet. "Oh, your poor
wrists—"

"It's nothing." Durant shaped tongue to a reply. "I'm not a
man to be held."

"God and liberty!" she cried. "And now we'll go on to my
uncle, to General Urrea, and then toward Cuba. I was lost in
the fog and stopped to rest. The horse will carry us both, Vicente.
You can ride? Good! The general shall know from you what
those Texas rebels are doing!"

At these words, Durant's frown cleared.

He had been baffled by this meeting. To take her horse and
go on, leaving her afoot—that was Vincent, but to him it was
impossible. To head the silly fool back to Gonzales and safety
would be hard.

But now Fate had tapped him on the shoulder with pointing
finger. Again the vengeance trail had forked. The larger mission
showed clear. Again he would cheat Vincent of the prey, and
still accomplish his errand. A fugitive from the enemy, in dis-
guise, vouched for by his companion—by Heaven, the way was
opened!

Urrea? Possible; even practicable. The dead man under the
bridge could no longer speak. Pedro Ortiz, the chatterbox,
would bear no tales, thanks to Vincent. There was a grim irony
in the whole situation.

Instead of being a courier from Santa Anna, Durant was a
fugitive from the Texas rebels. He could tell Urrea they were
swarming, accomplish Houston's purpose with ready tongue.

As for the casket, he knew the truth about it now—again, thanks to Vincent, who had gambled away the *doña's* jewels! The embezzled, stolen gold of Santa Anna—yes, there was his quarry! The game was fair. Thus Vincent should make restitution, and the old plantation should be again in the name of Durant.

HE BROKE into gusty laughter, and reached out his hand to the girl. "Come! We'll go on at once. As you desire."

"Then make the casket fast, Vicente—Oh, your poor wrists! Those terrible rebels shall pay for this!"

"Someone shall pay, at all events," said Durant. If she had anticipated more amorous greeting, he evaded it. A kiss, and she was satisfied to babble of the future.

The casket made fast again, they went on. The horse, trebly laden, made slow progress across the hours. Doña Amadora had a packet of food old Hittel had given her, and shared it. At least, it staved off hunger.

Durant was puzzled by the action of Hittel in turning off the girl in such fashion. Had Faith known? Or had it been done, perhaps, by Houston's order? Hardly; else some escort would have been sent. Perhaps there had actually been some talk of plundering Hittel's guest. There were plenty of rough characters in that camp at Gonzales.

All day they headed south with slow progress, none too certain of whereabouts, though sure enough of direction. With night or morning they were bound to strike the traveled road to their destination. As the day waned, Durant insensibly relaxed his harsh demeanor. The girl nestled here against him was a lovely thing, all woman; she deserved a better man than the real Vincent.

He treated her as a child confided to his care; thus in fact had destiny ruled the matter. Little she dreamed how good fortune had favored her, how she had slipped the snares of the real Vincent!

"She'll hate me in the end," and Durant shrugged at his own

thoughts. "What matters that? She'll hate me when she learns who killed her uncle. First, if I can turn her to serve Houston's purpose—all's well!"

No sign of habitation or settlement all that day. Darkness found them near a stream, with the usual night fog of this season rolling up again, but less thickly than the previous night.

They camped, made meager fare. They had no fire against the mist, and sheltered together beneath the poncho for warmth and life. Doña Amadora, pitched suddenly from luxury into hardship, had endured nobly to the point of utter exhaustion. She crept into Durant's arms with a sob, and was asleep before the sob was done. Poor child! He held her close, until slumber took quick toll of him.

They wakened to daylight, sun stripping the fog from brush and trees, and finished the last crumbs of food. Durant brought up the tethered horse, and with laughter and sunlit confidence prepared for the journey. They must strike a road soon, must be close upon it. All was well!

Durant was making fast the laced casket behind the saddle when he heard a startled cry from Doña Amadora. Then a voice broke in.

"*Buenos dias*, brother! Salutations, *señorita!*"

Durant stared at the man who had silently stepped from covert, stared with instant recognition. It was Jacopo, the lithe, tawny fellow of the bridge. And across his arm, warily, he carried his musketoon—cocked and ready.

CHAPTER VI

THE ONE-EYED PIPER

JACOPO UTTERED a shrill whistle.

The approach had been masterly. A second man made his appearance, leading horses. Durant saw that flight was out of the question.

"*Buenos dias,*" he rejoined. "What do you want, *amigo?*"

Jacopo's gaze flitted to the chest, balanced but still untied behind the saddle. By his jaunty, easy mien and his *caballero's* velvet costume, he might have been a friend of old acquaintance. His thin lips smiled over the widely set teeth.

"What I see you have, brother," he rejoined. "Very good. You are a man of honor. I must admit that our captain was getting somewhat alarmed, hence he scattered us out to search for you. I assured him that you'd make no mistakes, and so I see. Permit me to give you a hand, brother," and he approached. "I hope the thing is heavy—"

Doña Amadora perceived his intent.

"Bandits!" she cried out. "The chest—you shall not touch it. Do you rob women, *señor?* It is mine; it holds nothing of value. Beware what you do, insolent! I am Doña Amadora de la Vega, and if you molest us you shall be punished!"

Vain words, after the way of a woman, thought Durant. But at these words the brows of Jacopo lifted. He shot a glance at Durant, a glance of significance, of startled but honest admiration. Then he swept off his silvered sombrero to the girl.

"De la Vega? How curious! I know the name very well; it

reminds me of an adventure I once had," and he grinned at Durant. "My poor name, *señorita*, is a mere Jacopo, not worthy to be mentioned in the same breath with yours. You may look upon me as a man of honor, like this *caballero* whom you favor. Nothing of yours shall be harmed. We have merely come to escort you upon a little errand."

The girl hesitated upon him, half doubting, half believing. Not so Durant.

"Enough of this, Jacopo!" he exclaimed. "Your captain's nothing to me; I don't know him. The lady and I are riding south on private business. Get out. We don't want your escort."

"Indeed?" Clapping hat to head, Jacopo sardonically laid finger to nose. "A mistake, no doubt; I take the blame, *caballero*. Once you've explained to the captain, you'll be sent on your way unharmed. My word on it! Our captain has a heart for romance, and he's a most human fellow."

By now Doña Amadora caught the note of mockery.

"Oh, this is intolerable!" She whirled on Durant. "You're an officer, Vicente—can you do nothing? Must we submit to this brigand?"

Durant stood impassive. He had already noted that the second man, lounging in his saddle, held a ready pistol.

"Alas, my *doña*"—it was Jacopo who made response—"I fear you must. A brave man, this *caballero* of yours, but—" He tapped his musketoon. With a clucking sound, he drew thumb across throat and grinned. "It'd be a pity. If you insist, of course we'll put a knife into him, merely to exhibit the fact of his courage—"

"*Santo Dios!*" burst out the girl wildly. "You are a devil! We'll go with you. End this nonsense. Submit, Vicente, submit!"

"Well and wisely said," approved Jacopo, and he bowed to Durant. "You hear, *compañero?* Your wrists, I see, are hurt. Permit me to aid you; I'll take care of the casket on my own horse. Come along there, Juan!"

THE SECOND man brought up the horses. Jacopo lifted the casket to his own animal and made it fast. He slung the

*"Shall it be the quick
knife, here and now?"*

musketoon over his back and got into the saddle. From a holster
he lifted a pistol and placed it in his sash.

"Now, *caballero*, you shall sit your horse alone," he exclaimed.
"You and I will ride together. The lady will share the saddle of
my companion, who has a strong horse, and who is a man of
honor. Come! No protests, I beg of you. Juan, assist the *doña*
to the saddle!"

Helpless, Doña Amadora complied. Durant, torn by chagrin,
anger, futility, kept silence. Once again, he perceived, the dead
man was indeed speaking. With that meeting by the half-
sunken bridge, destiny had snared him in a net there was no
escaping. He must, for the sake of his mission, for the sake of
his own honor at the end, have patience. He himself might get
away, but he could not desert this girl.

He mounted and rode off beside Jacopo, who kept a wary
eye on him.

"*Diantre*, brother!" said the rascal, striking out well ahead of
the other two on the single horse. "The gold and a lady; the one
to deliver, the other to keep, eh? You're a proper comrade; I

salute you! All can be arranged. We'll be just in time, with damned little to spare. The captain's eye is smoldering. You had difficulties, eh?"

"Yes," Durant said, tight-lipped.

"The *calabozo*; I've heard about it. But there was help. And later?"

"We met Texans on the road. They took us to Gonzales, prisoners."

"Ho! That explains your chafed wrists. And you yet got away, gold, lady and all! Again I salute you. Well, the captain's a man of business; all's well that ends well. You are bringing the gold, I take it?"

"The casket speaks," snapped Durant.

"Assuredly. The *señorita* does not know, eh?"

Durant shook his head. Jacopo grinned.

"And she, of the de la Vega family—a daughter, a niece! *Caramba!* You're a clever one. You give with one hand and take with the other; a true Brother of the Blade. And born to fortune. You raise the needful, you have friends at hand to help you out of a pinch, you make away with the *pesos de oro* and a willing beauty, you suffer for love and honor! And in the nick of time you're rescued again from adversity and taken on to your destination without the least bother to yourself. Hang it, those who are lucky win at cards!"

The jaunty voice had the bite of sarcasm, of hidden innuendo. Durant felt the cold breath of peril chill the nape of his neck. He made no response to the banter, and having said his say, Jacopo fell silent.

The noonday sun brought their ride to an end.

An outspread camp appeared in a clump of scrub timber near the verge of a small, willowed stream. Three brush huts denoted some permanency here.

Picketed horses and mules, the thin fumes of mesquite wood, sprawled, lazying men, half a dozen in number. Studied gaze from eyes brim-shaded but glinting; the curling drift of corn-husk cigarettes poised at lips, a ringing shout from Jacopo.

"God and liberty! *Viva, caballeros!* We are come and all is well!" He motioned to Durant. "Come, brother—to the captain!"

Durant met seeming recognition and greetings from the men, waved his hand, and rode on to the hut where Jacopo halted and swung to earth.

BEFORE THE hut, seated in thin shade upon a cowhide, was a man, immensely hatted, immensely bearded, immensely bulked. Of slovenly aspect in dirty shirt, belt-less pantaloons sagging from his paunch, grimy bare feet spread to the air, matted hair and beard uncombed by brush or fingers. In hairy front and in bulk a very buffalo of a man, blackly, ferociously visaged, and with a single eye.

But what an eye! A veritable jewel in a dunghill; like burnished jet, gleaming diamond-bright from the thicket of its overhanging brows. An unwinking eye, a steadily glowing planet of an eye that, answering for two eyes, saw everything.

At sight of Doña Amadora dismounting and being led to him, El Tuerto, with an amazing agility, sprang to straddled legs and plucked off his hat. A grimacing smile contorted his features.

"A lady? Do I see a lady in this rude camp? Marvelous! It is too much honor!"

The voice was a squeak. It issued from an absurdly small and rosy mouth; the smile revealed a setting of pearly, boyish little teeth. The round, pouty mouth was a punctuation mark between those broad and heavy chops. And somehow, past understanding, the voice, mouth and teeth were more fearsome than the disgusting bulk, the hairy visage, the planet eye.

"A seat for the lady! Peons, cowherds! Are you gentlemen or savages?"

The voice shrilled with signs of power. Men leaped into motion, scurried about. One of them came at the dead run with a low cowhide stool. Jacopo presented it to Doña Amadora with a bow. White, eyes startled, she sank upon it.

"With your permission," squeaked El Tuerto, and with a sigh of the flesh he settled himself at ease again. He cocked his bright orb at the sun, then flashed it at Durant. "Hm! Slightly overdue, *caballero*. Well, Jacopo?"

"*Señor capitan*, the lady delayed us somewhat," said Jacopo, betraying a semblance of very real respect. "Our honest brother had a misadventure or two. However, we have what you expected. Here it comes."

The man Juan was bringing the chest. He deposited it before the one-eyed, who prodded it with a bare, grimy foot and made comment.

"My toes say '*muy bien.*' I trust they don't lie; if so, someone shall suffer." His one eye rolled upon Durant, pierced like a long blade, then shortened as though satisfied. He went on in his mouse voice: "We will wait, for better enjoyment. Some fools would rush to verify, to make sure, to gaze upon the litter. Not I! Such a thing is to be enjoyed in fancy. The lady, our guest, needs refreshment and rest."

Doña Amadora bridled under his gaze.

"I am Doña Amadora de la Vega!" she exclaimed. "And you? How do you call yourself?"

The captain whistled softly and turned quizzical eye upon Durant. Evidently he had heard the story of Jacopo regarding the scene by the bridge, long ere this.

"De la Vega! And she is yours, *caballero?* Ah, what a devil of a fellow you are! You do us all credit. We, alas, get only the gold." He sighed. Then, with his monstrous, unexpected nimbleness, he gained his legs and bowed to the lady. "*Señorita*, I can make but a poor return for such an honored name as yours. You behold, at your service, Captain Don Tio Innocencio Nevado y Esperador. To command!"

Whereupon "Uncle Innocence Snow-white and Hopeful"

was fain to reseat himself with legs extended. He gestured curtly to Durant.

"Brother Vicente, attend the *doña* to the next hut, there. It is hers in privacy. Refreshments will be sent her. You yourself return here for discussion of campaign."

D U R A N T   T O O K the girl's hand and led her to the brush shelter adjoining. At the entrance she turned, her liquid eyes, wide with alarm, seeking his face.

"Vicente, I am afraid of that man, of all these men. They know you?"

"It's all a mistake," said Durant quietly. "I don't think you'll be harmed."

"But you—it is for you I fear! They're bandits, they'll want ransom; they talk of gold. He shall have the casket, then; tell him to take it, and let us go."

Durant nodded, reassured her, and turned back.

El Tuerto was sitting ponderous, flaccid, amiable and bright of eye. The casket had not been touched, in its canvas casing.

"Now to business, Vicente," he piped. "I'll say nothing about your being a trifle overdue. And then, there was the lady. Doña de la Vega, says she. So you're excused, my son. But there's one little, trifling matter to settle between us. You've brought the gold—"

"One moment," cut in Durant. "As to the gold, may it lodge in your gullet, chest and all! Now, for whom do you take me?"

The bright eye fixed on him and pierced.

"For an honest man, my bravo; or else for a dead rascal." The cruel puppy-teeth shone in smile. "It looks to me as though you had tasted a sore throat already. Yes, you broach the very point. Do I take you for my honest recruit Vicente, formerly of the army?

"Or do I take you for one who forgets his duty to his captain, and brings in a ravishing beauty whom he intends to keep for himself?"

Durant frowned. So this mountain of flesh was touched by
the girl, eh?

"Clear up this mistake," he said abruptly. "I'm not your recruit.
He's my half-brother, Vicente Durant; we look much alike. You
and Jacopo made the error. Have it understood without further
delay. You never saw me before, nor I you."

El Tuerto quivered with mirth, and suddenly altered his
mood to one of cunning.

"So that's it, eh? What the devil!" His flashing eye darted
toward the adjacent cabin. "She does not know, eh? She thinks—
ha! *Caspita!* You're a clever devil! All right, then; I yield her to
you. All is understood between us. I never saw you before,
brother! She shall find out nothing from me."

"The devil!" burst out Durant with angry exasperation. "You
have it all wrong, you accursed fool! I tell you—"

"Enough! Guard your tongue." El Tuerto lifted himself a
little. His voice took on sudden power, his eye took on menace.
"You've said all, and so have I. She's yours, and that ends it.
Now get yourself something to eat and let's have peace. This is
the siesta hour. When it's over," and his one eye caressed the
canvas-covered casket, "we'll open the gold. It won't take wings
while it's between my feet. Off with you!"

The eye closed. The monster leaned back, sighed luxuri-
ously, and gurgled himself to sleep.

Durant limped away; he was startled by the real power of
this fleshly lump, so hintingly revealed. No fool, this rascal!

Joining the other men, he commandeered meat and drink,
of which there was plenty, then stretched out in a patch of shade.
He could do nothing else. While the camp seemed to be enjoy-
ing siesta, he sensed that every movement of his was noted from
between drooped lids. What to do? Unless he wanted to chance
escape and leave the girl here he could do nothing.

He slept.

"COME, *VALIENTES!* Come, my little doves! Gather

around me, *caballeros*, gentlemen, heroes all! Brethren of the Blade, *compañeros* of the trail to me!"

The voice roused Durant. Surprising strength in its pipe and squeak; significant also. One should not take El Tuerto at face value, as grew more evident all the while.

Siesta had passed. The sun was midway of its western arc. The captain, bawling with impatience, was sitting up with legs spraddled and the casket between them, against the bulge of paunch. He was the very semblance of an ape with a coconut.

The men alertly sauntered in, to seat themselves in a half-circle about him. Doña Amadora appeared at the entrance to her brush shelter, hesitant. El Tuerto beckoned to Durant, saw her and repeated the gesture with fat and hairy forefinger.

"Come, my *caballero*, brother Vicente, on my left! Our *doña* on my right, to queen it over us. *Señorita*, you will regard me as an aunt rather than as an uncle—your Tia Innocencia of happy memory."

Doña Amadora stood straitly before him, with level gaze and cool accusation. "Then you steal my casket, you unspeakable brigand?"

"No, no, *mi chiquita!*" purled the captain. "Only the contents, I assure you. We count on the generosity of your lovely self, of your noble *caballero*. Have I permission, and perhaps a key?"

"You wish ransom, in other words?" she retorted with hauteur. "Very well, there it is. If I swear to you that the contents of that casket will make you rich, do you swear upon the Cross that I and this gentleman, Captain Don Vicente Durant, shall at once go free and these bandits of yours?"

"My heart assures me," and El Tuerto, smirking, laid paw to dirty breast, "that such a lovely mouth could speak only truth. But this eye of mine—it is a damned unholy eye—insists upon satisfaction for itself. And being my only eye, I favor it. Let's grant it one little look; and then, as God hears me, if my eye says 'Yes,' you and your *caballero* shall depart." He sighed ponderously. "In any event, your going leaves me the poorer. Ah, the woman, the woman! I too have loved—"

"God has heard," cut in the girl coldly. "Open the chest. Here's the key," and drawing from her bosom a key on a ribbon, she flung it down at him.

DURANT WATCHED and listened, frowningly intent, but helpless. When she found gold instead of her jewels—then what? Well, the gold was gone now, and the quicker he got away from here with her, the better.

"Truly a key to treasure!" El Tuerto's huge paw swooped on the key. He addressed the half-circle of seated men. "Now we seal the bargain. This *caballero*, this utter stranger," and he gestured to Durant, "who with his lady has been brought to us by a most astonishing mistake—a mistake, my *valientes*—is rewarding our hospitality by making us a little gift. As men of honor we will send them on with our blessing. But first—patience, all. The matter is delicate, but hunger sweetens the meal."

With huge fingers, amazingly supple, he plucked at the thongs lacing the canvas cover. The tip of his greedy tongue parted his lips; he was suddenly absorbed and intent. So were the watching half-circle of men. Eyes glowed, like the eyes of wolves watching and waiting for the pack king to gorge upon the kill.

The lacings of the canvas came loose. The canvas was opened and slipped off, to reveal the leathern casket. Tooled leather of Spanish work. And now the key; to the hiss of indrawn breaths it entered the lock. At the first touch, it seemed, the clasp of brass flew open.

"Ha! A lock too willing!" piped El Tuerto, and flung the lid open. He raked inside with one hairy paw. "Thunders of God!"

It was a bellow that came belching through the funnel of his mouth. The chest contents flew wide—pebbles, clay, fragments of iron showered the ground. Another roar, a lift of the ponderous body, a kick. The chest went rolling, gaped emptily to the sky. Stones, clay, iron—nothing else.

In that instant of silence, the shocked brain of Durant wakened to life. He glimpsed the figure of old Hittel, Faith's father, urging the *doña* on her way; the figure smirked of greed and cunning. He had pillaged the chest, had refilled it with weight of dross to match, had sent Doña Amadora on her way with hasty story—

And now to pay the piper. The one-eyed piper.

CHAPTER VII

LEY DE FUGA

DOÑA AMADORA sprang up in stark amaze, white-faced, eyes staring large.

"My jewels!" her voice lifted and shrilled. "The casket contained my jewels, those of my mother, my family! There is some mistake—"

"Mistake!" The word came with a hiss from the half-circle of men, and El Tuerto echoed it, repeated it. "Mistake! And you! You?"

This at Durant, with flaming eye of reptilian menace, a deadly eye now.

"Not I," Durant said vehemently. "The gold is gone. In Gonzales—"

"The gold?" Before anyone else could cut in, Doña Amadora whirled upon him, took the word with blazing energy.

"Gold, you say? What gold? Vicente, have you tricked me? The jewels were yours; they were ours. Yours for the asking. When I heard a story that you had stolen gold of the government, I laughed at it. Was that why you were arrested? Where are my jewels?"

All eyes settled upon the two of them, every ear was intent. Durant met the moment squarely, without pretense.

"Take the truth, even if it hurts, then," he said curtly. "I never saw the inside of that chest. I never saw you before that day we met in the plaza at Bejar. I am not Vicente at all. I am Gordon Durant, his half-brother. You mistook me, these men have

77

mistaken me. What the chest contained was none of my doing. That scoundrel Vicente sold your jewels at the monte games, replaced them with his stolen gold."

The harsh, uncompromising words fell upon silence. Of them all, perhaps Doña Amadora doubted the least, believed the most. But not El Tuerto.

"So, he never saw the inside of that chest before—what a pity he's here to see it now!" purred the captain, with restraint of choked fury. "Yes; the lady is of shorter acquaintance with him than she thought. He is not Captain Don Vicente, he did not change the jewels to gold, the gold to dirt—ho! But the lady has been robbed, and we, who are honest men, have been robbed. Well, this passes a joke!" His voice lifted in a roaring gust of sound, deepening in tone as he shouted. "Who is this fellow, my *valientes?*"

The half-circle of "valiant men" grinned, and made chorused answer.

"He's Vicente Durant, my captain!"

"Wait—you do not understand!" The shocked and horrified gaze of Doña Amadora turned from Durant. She faced El Tuerto, appealingly, but the monstrous captain wagged his beard and broke in upon her.

"I understand better than you think, lady. It is for you to wait. We do things here in due form, by process of law; we are honest men. *Compañeros!* Is this Vicente Durant a sworn brother of the Blade?"

"He was, my captain."

"And why is he no longer?"

"He cheated the brethren at cards, my captain," came the chorus, fiercely.

"What sentence was passed upon him?"

"That to save his throat he should pay us ten thousand *pesos* in gold, my captain."

"Has he done so?"

"No!" The chorused yell was rabid, shrill.

"Then he has broken his vow?"

"Yes!" Louder and shriller the yell.

"And what is the penalty?"

"The knife, my captain, the knife!" came response.

EL TUERTO spread out his hands. "You see, the matter is out of my hands," he announced. "Crime begets punishment. There is no more to be said; somewhat to be done. Those who swear by the knife, and fail, perish by the knife. No appeals, Vicente?"

Durant met the fire-filled thrust of that staring, brooding eye, and shrugged.

"I've told you I'm not Vicente; that's all."

"He's merely Vicente's twin," and El Tuerto chuckled. "Unluckily for him, gold has no twin."

"*Señor*, I think you are honest," said Doña Amadora, with simple dignity, looking Durant in the face. "At Gonzales, you say? Yes; you've acted the *caballero*. We've traveled together," and her eyes softened. "They shall not kill you! Do you hear?" And swiftly she swung upon El Tuerto. "You shall have the gold! You shall have it!"

The burning eye of the captain rested upon her.

"How is that, lady?"

"I'll get it for you," she cried eagerly, passionately. "You were promised ten thousand dollars, you say? This man is not the one you think him, he's under no promise to you; all the same, you shall be paid ransom."

"Excellent, my *doña!*" lisped the captain, in imitation of her Castilian. "Twenty thousand in gold. Ten thousand was the price of a rascal. We wouldn't insult this honest *caballero* who tells us he's not the rascal. Twenty thousand."

Doña Amadora bit her lip. Durant, on fire with her words, her look, burst into the talk hotly.

"You're dealing with a low scoundrel; have done! He'll gain nothing by killing me, or by keeping me. The gold is gone and so's the rascal. Let this fat pig do as he pleases. You're to go, without wasting words on him."

"The ten thousand is in Gonzales, you say?" queried El Tuerto softly.

"Was, not is," rasped Durant. Vincent? Perhaps; let them trail him. But not Faith's father. This beast and his far-handed brotherhood should not be put on that scent. "You'll get no gold there."

"If the lady thinks to go there, it's a long journey," observed El Tuerto. "And there's the extra ten thousand as well. We must have it in three days."

Doña Amadora spoke bravely, defying Durant with a pale smile that overbore his words and entreaties.

"Four days, and you'll have the money. I don't go to Gonzales, but to San Patricio. I must have time."

"To San Patricio!" mused El Tuerto. "And what will happen there?"

"I'll see my uncle. He'll find the ransom; you shall be paid."

Durant felt himself gripped by an icy horror. The situation was past his ordering; it was running to a conclusion he could not prevent.

"And who the devil is this uncle? If he can hatch out twenty thousand *pesos* he's worth knowing!"

"He is Captain Don Leon Victorio de la Vega," she declaimed proudly. "He is rich, his word is good, he can borrow if he lacks. He is my guardian, and keeps any pledge I may make. When I ask him for the life of this *caballero*, he will assent."

THE TOES of El Tuerto ceased to wriggle. His pouty mouth rounded into a perfect O of astonishment. His voice came like a squeal of sarcasm.

"*Hombre!* What love for a *caballero!* And you really are a de la Vega? No, no, my lady. Your worthy uncle shall rest in peace. When it comes to money, I've small faith in prayers."

"Prayers?" she repeated. Durant, listening, felt the cold chill draw closer. "I tell you he'll listen to me—"

"He's probably busy," cut in El Tuerto, grinning. "But if he hears you, he'll say that he needs the money to get him out of purgatory. *Diantre!* First you'd trick me with a casket of rubbish. Now you pledge ransom with a coffin of the same stuff."

"A coffin?" she repeated, drawing herself up, yet perplexed.

"A coffin, I say!" roared the other shrilly. "This *caballero* knocked your uncle on the head in the Arroyo Hondo and then joined you in Bejar. But I see I'll get no gold. Jacopo! Reassure the lady. We're honest men here, all but one of us!"

Jacopo stood up, jaunty and assured, and gave Durant a grin.

"It is true," he said to the staring, transfixed girl. "I was there. I saw it done, and very well done, upon my word. One crack with a pistol-butt! I helped Vicente chuck the body under the arroyo bridge. He took the uniform and rode on to Bejar for the gold. He said nothing about a lady—"

His words carried weight. Doña Amadora swung around and her eyes drove at Durant with questioning horror.

"You!" She breathed the one word. Durant inclined his head slightly.

"It is quite true," he said steadily, quietly. "You see, I had never met you then. Not that it would have made any difference. He threatened me; I took the pistol away from him and struck—too hard. Later, I could not tell you the truth, until I had seen you in safety."

No more to be said, and no less. El Tuerto chuckled.

"*Vaya!* Perhaps these twin brethren are two in one, eh? He tells a good tale."

Doña Amadora had not taken her eyes from Durant's face. They dilated; her cheeks were very white.

"I gave you my name; you companioned me," she said slowly. The welling horror in her voice gripped every ear, every eye. "I see it all now. The stolen gold replacing my jewels. The uniform of Tampico—ah, *Dios!* My uncle's uniform! And at Gonzales you traded the gold for liberty. You had that man send me away with the worthless chest. You followed and found me—God knows what you would have done before we reached San Patricio!"

Durant stood thunderstruck at the plausible piecing together of evidence. Conviction rang firmer in her voice. Suddenly she whipped around.

"He sold himself to the rebels!" she cried out. "He would have played spy in San Patricio—that was it! He's a coward and a traitor. Kill him! Kill him! I wouldn't give a single hair to save his life!"

Durant remained motionless, impassive now. Somehow she had divined the truth.

"An excellent idea," approved El Tuerto.

"Be careful! He'll escape!" she flamed. "You don't know him!"

EL TUERTO chuckled at this. "No? Another excellent idea there. The *ley de fuga.*" A murmur of eager approval came from the other men. He cocked his one eye at the westering sun. "Too late today. It must be tomorrow: You will remain, *doña?* It will be worth seeing, I can tell you."

"He is already carrion to me," she said disdainfully. "I want to leave now, at once! I go to the army of General Urrea at San Patricio."

"Very well; you shall have safe escort, and you'll kindly present my compliments to the general." El Tuerto wagged his great beard, and beckoned the man who had helped Jacopo bring the two into camp. "Juan, my son! Take one of the brethren whom you may select, and escort this lady to San Patricio. See to her safety and comfort. Go!"

Juan motioned to another man, who rose and accompanied him. El Tuerto swept his hand out toward the others.

"My *valientes!* The mistakes have all been explained. Shall it be the quick knife, here and now, or shall he make the last mistake of the *ley de fuga!*"

"*Bueno, bueno!*" arose the swift eager voice. "*Ley de fuga!*"

"In the morning, then. Let him rest tonight and meditate on his sins. Take him away."

Durant was seized and propelled into the same brush hut lately vacated by Doña Amadora; bound, not too tightly, and left to his own meditations.

The law of flight? Whatever it portended, it had a smell of hope.

Die? He had not sought this Texas to be killed with his errand unfinished. There was yet vengeance to be had on Vincent. And Faith—in those blue eyes he would yet see gladness in place of scorn!

What the devil was Vincent doing now? There was gold in Gonzales, gold from the Mexican war chest, a weapon to be used in the conquest of the new Texan Republic. Ten thousand dollars; the sum was still due him. The gold was rightfully for him and Faith and their future, and so it should be.

No, he did not foresee death on the morrow. He slept, with the cords burning his wrists and ankles to remind him of the value of courage, and with the vision of Faith brooding above him as assurance of hope.

And while he lay, in the bonds of petty personal fortune, across the night sky and the prairies were sweeping the gathering events of destiny. Doña Amadora rode south with her escort and so out of the story, and Captain Desauque, upon a lame and hobbling horse, moved unwittingly to bring about his share in bloody horror that was to sweep aside all thought of that lesser tragedy in the Alamo.

So came the morning again.

Durant was freed of his bonds and brought forth. The sunlight flooded a camp gay with chatter and expectancy. Animals were being prepared, equipment overhauled; the hunters were getting ready for the kill. Long lances, brought by deserters from some Mexican cavalry contingent, were being whetted to cruel iron points.

Obese and blowsy, El Tuerto sat upon his cowhide in the warming beams, as though he had not moved since the previous evening. Durant was led before him, and the *valientes* gathered about with lances and pistols. The worthy captain set forth the order of the day. He himself, it appeared, was not sharing in the festivity.

"On the word of a Christian," he assured Durant benevolently, "you shall escape—if you can. By the *ley de fuga* you must take the consequences. You shall have freedom of two hundred paces before the others are let loose upon you. A generous opportunity."

"Thanks," Durant said drily. "And then? You mean I'm to run for it?"

EL TUERTO pursed his baby mouth. "Well, if you get away, you're gone. If you don't get away, you're dead. I know that you're resolved on escape; so much the better, if you make it. You should be grateful. We might have slit your throat, in which case you'd have no breath to run with."

"As I'd like to slit yours," said Durant impassively. El Tuerto shook his head.

"Blood! The sight of it sickens me, my dear brother. I was intended for a butcher, but whenever I stuck a sheep I lost my last meal."

"You'll lose more than that if I get a chance at you," Durant said grimly.

"And so, as one trained to nobility," smugly pursued El Tuerto, "mercy and the dread of violence move me to wait upon your escape. How goes it, my *valientes?* Are you ready?"

"Ready, my captain!" Lance-points glittered in the sunlight. Eight-foot cavalry lances, heavy of haft, keen of blade, wound with thongs for better grip.

"Here, two of you! This *caballero* is bent upon escaping in the clothes God gave him. He can thus slip through the brush so much faster! Come, my brave one. Will you prepare for escape, or shall these honest fellows prepare you? They're clever at it."

Durant glanced about. No help for it. Horses were being brought up; behind the raillery of the captain lurked eager cruelty. With a shrug, he removed his clothes and stood naked; and at a commanding gesture, barefoot. What matter? He was not to die this day. He had resolved upon it.

"A fine figure of a man. When I was younger, I was like that myself," and El Tuerto nodded, fingering the knife at his belt. "Now for the orders. Two hundred paces—it will bring you to the brush yonder, just this side the creek, at the bend."

He pointed to the curving creek, with unbroken chaparral stretching away into the distance across the water and green willows.

"You have all that brush before you, in which you can run about like a rabbit. And I give you the word of a *caballero*," he squeaked, "that if you reach the other side of the brush, the hunt is ended. It is not more than half a league; two miles at the most. No lack of cover, eh? Nothing to a man with your legs."

Durant comprehended fully. In that brush he was to take cover, naked, and these others would hunt him down with lance and pistol, as pigs were hunted. Escape? Not a chance of it. No hiding behind mesquite branches. Those lances would reach into brush and prick him forth. Good sport!

"One moment, my *valientes!*" El Tuerto grunted himself to his bare feet and waddled into the brush shelter. He emerged again, holding up garments with admiration. Voices broke forth from the men.

"A prize!" he announced. "Men do not ride hard for nothing. And these rags of Don Vicente's—pouf! They're not fit for gentlemen. Here are *botas, calzones, chaqueta*, worthy any *caballero!* They go to the man who brings me the rabbit's ears—both ears. But they must be taken in the brush, understand well. If he gets into the open beyond, he's safe. Understood?"

"Understood, my captain," came the chorus, like the yapping of dogs.

Tanned, fanciful, stitched boots soft as leggings; blue velvet jacket with silver buttons, black velvet pantaloons buttoned with silver buckles at the hips. And a crimson waist-sash. El Tuerto deposited them in a heap at one side, then deposited himself again, with a sigh, on his cowhide.

"N O W F O R it!" he said affably to Durant. "Do you need a lance prick, or do you take to the road without regrets?"

"With only one regret," Durant said calmly. "I must postpone slitting your belly."

"Splendid, from a man whose chest flutters like the throat of a bird in the net!" El Tuerto leaned back. "Go for it, *caballero!* Until you plunge into the brush, I'll hold back these gentle doves of mine—but don't delay over-long, I advise you."

Durant turned and walked away, gratified that his heart was steady as his voice. He was aware that each man now stood by his saddle, lance in hand, ready to mount and be after him at the word. He did not look at them; his eyes drove ahead.

The way for him lay northward, up the course of the stream, until he should reach the bend. The scrub timber of the camp, thinned out for firewood, soon ended. Mulberries and willows screened the creek. Out beyond the chaparral stretched to the west and north in a harsh jungle grown as high as a man's head, and it gave place to the bared Texas plain on beyond—if he could make it.

He walked with measured pace, but now his muscles were tightening, his eyes were searching the cover ahead. Once across the stream there was cover enough; it was tempting to the eye. Yet a naked man would find short shrift there against the plunge of horse and the thrust of lance.

He heard never a sound, save his own heartbeats. His steps shortened; he came to a pause. Here was the bound before him. Quick eyes probed the ground. Then, with a leap like that of a frightened buck, he was into the cover and into the water beyond, and heard the joyous yells of the unleashed pack behind.

Half across the creek, while yet the thunderous hooves

behind were but growing, he sighted a narrow wash upstream, canopied by dead brush. Narrow, but deep enough. He took it headlong, careless of the hedging branches that snatched at his bare flesh, and went burrowing deep. Then he lay still, motionless.

With yelp and yell the pursuit came on, horses racing and splashing across the creek above and below him, crashing into the brush beyond. Mud and water splashed him as a horse vaulted the narrow wash. The riot passed on, no doubt to spread widely, circle about the stretch of brush, and then quarter back to prevent his escape.

Terror ripped at him. The shrill whir of a rattlesnake was vibrating through his head; lodged somewhere in the narrow wash, invisible to him. The signal of a sounding snake, coiled in covert, is illusive as a bat in the twilight. The sibilant roll of sound rang alarm. Other ears might hear. Cursing the snake, Durant backed his way out.

He wakened now. Indian cunning took hold of him; he thought of the camp and El Tuerto squatting there like an ape scratching his shins. While the hunters kept to the brush, he would keep to the stream. If the way north were closed, he might head to the south—not through the brush, but downstream and in opposite ways.

Stooping low, scanning the brush around, he gained the water and silently made his way downstream, watchful for any crashing horseman. The bend lay ahead. He was already at it when he stopped, foot upraised. The *plosh-plosh* of hooves in water was coming toward him. He glanced about—no cover, except the leafy green beside him. He writhed in amongst it, parted the screen ahead, peered out.

THERE WAS the jaunty, tawny gallant, Jacopo himself, eyes cruelly alight, mouth pursed, lance at work. Shrewder than the others, Jacopo was prodding the leafy depths along the stream, and doing it thoroughly, his long lance reaching in with snaky tongue, jabbing down to flush the covert, advancing again.

And it was close, coming closer each instant. Durant cowered, gathered his muscles. His hands poised, fingers tensed. Jacopo was within three feet of him now. The lance drove in, a yard away, explored, lifted out again. It shoved down—straight at him this time—

Like the swift strike of a water-moccasin, Durant's hands gripped the shaft of the lance as it descended. Gripped it, jerked it with all his weight upon it. Taken completely by surprise, the man in the saddle came down with the lance, toppling so swiftly that he had no chance for outcry. The tinseled sombrero fell. Jacopo himself fell, and the fingers of Durant clamped in upon his throat.

He thrashed for a little, but the hard hands had him. One hand to chin, the other to breast. Twist—back again, shoulder-thews in the jerk! There was a click, a dull crunch. The body relaxed and went limp.

Here was the flashing moment—not an instant to waste now! The pursuit, the hue and cry, was afield in the brush. Durant caught up the hat, the lance, scrambled naked into saddle, kicked his heels into the horse's ribs.

On the cowhide before the brush hut, El Tuerto sprawled lazily supine, inert, his one eye basking sleepily in the sunlight. The *thump-thump* of hoofbeats rolled along the ground. His half-shut orb flew open, then distended on the sight of naked man, hatted, lance poised in hand, riding upon him like an avenging fury.

With inarticulate cry, El Tuerto heaved his monstrous form toward erectness, but never stood upon those bare feet of his again. He clutched, vainly, as the glittering tongue of steel drove in. The lance-point parted his matted beard, sped home through throat and neck.

Durant reined in, wheeled the animal swiftly, and came back. The heavy shaft of the lance had toppled over sideways, bearing the fallen bulk of flesh with it. Durant slipped from the saddle, seized the lance, wrenched it free.

Now for the clothes, to cover his galled and scalded body.

No time for other loot. He swung up into the saddle again; the fine soft boots pinched his feet, but he was not one to look a gift horse out of countenance. Whither? Not for Gonzales; those others would expect such course, would spur after him. Vincent, Faith, Houston—these were of a future once more deferred. His errand? Useless. Doña Amadora was with Urrea, and the specter of Captain de la Vega warned him away.

Goliad, then—Goliad and Fannin, whom he had left on useless mission! Head for Victoria or Goliad to the eastward and the south! The horse swung about. The boot-heels drove in.

CHAPTER VIII

A DESPERATE STAND

SUNSET APPROACHING, and a road, a muddy road. And horsemen to the eastward.

Durant conned road and men, warily. He conjectured this must be the road between Victoria to the east and Goliad to his west. The horsemen were coming from Victoria, then. No uniforms. Texas volunteers, perhaps. Durant drew rein, waiting. He saw scouts tearing out in advance, and he still waited.

His confidence dwindled suddenly. A rifle puffed, and the ball whistled past. Another shot; he took swift alarm. He had forgotten his own costume. He was here posed with lance and garb like a Mexican vedette! Those men had the Alamo in their hearts and guns in their hands; bullets were impatient of parley.

With flourish of uplifted palm, he wheeled his horse about, put heels to ribs and head to the breeze, and went galloping for the safer precincts of Goliad. Their mounts were no doubt weary, for he outran them quickly enough at full larrup.

A horseman in the road ahead had been waiting with pistol out, warned by the shots. Durant's horse was hard on the bit and not to be turned; full strength on the reins brought the animal sliding to its haunches. The pistol was lowered, and Captain Desauque, from Gonzales, broke into a gay laugh.

"Well met, well met! And in time. The man in the general's tent, eh? My bullet was for the garb and not for the face—luckily, I have good sight."

Durant struck hands and told of the horsemen behind. Horton's cavalry, no doubt—a band of thirty men on forced march from Matagorda to join Colonel Fannin at Goliad. Together he and Desauque, who was French or Spanish by his name, turned westward.

"I'm late, but not too late, I trust," Desauque said. "Soft trails and a lamed horse, a remount found with difficulty—that explains it. The ranches are poor in stock and afraid to lend. What of you? This costume?"

Durant laughed. "I fell among thieves," he said, and told of El Tuerto and the law of flight. He cut it to bare narrative, omitting private affairs. "So I collected payment for my own ears and left him with throat open to the sun."

"Good lance, good deed!" exclaimed Desauque. "I've heard of that scoundrel. And you say there was a woman in the camp who saw you and was released for San Patricio? Then take warning, and abandon your errand. Well, Fannin will have my dispatch before dark; there's Goliad ahead. From what I've picked up, Urrea has been reinforced. If Fannin doesn't retire instantly, Urrea will be on him; that man is a very mine of energy."

The San Antonio river was belted with low timber. On the western side the village of Goliad was overlooked by the gray stone walls of the presidio, the Mission of the Holy Ghost, inland from the Bay of the Holy Ghost—La Bahia del Espiritu Santo. Hence the confusion of names given the place, indifferently Goliad or La Bahia.

Above the church floated the flag of Ward's Georgia Battalion. A white flag of silk, bearing a large blue star, and the motto: "Where Liberty Dwells, There Is Our Country." The mission had become a fortress, the strongest in Texas outside San Antonio.

The two men rode in. Sentries greeted, men came running, here was Colonel Fannin striding out to grip hands cordially with Durant.

"So you didn't find Travis. There's nothing to say; I know the worst. Captain Desauque? Welcome to Fort Defiance; our new name for the old place. Come in, Durant, gentlemen—eh? A dispatch?"

FANNIN HAD thinned, bore a look of care and worry, but his carriage was gallant as ever. Report had it that West Point had given him military training. He tore at the letter Desauque handed him. As he read it, his face became older, grayer; a light of desperation filled his eyes. He looked up, crushed the dispatch in his hand.

"No," he said. "No! Captain King's company were sent to bring off the settlers from Refugio. They were attacked. Colonel Ward's battalion were sent to reinforce King. Nothing has been heard from since; not a messenger has come back." He paused. Durant understood suddenly the torment that wrenched at his soul.

Houston had ordered him to retreat instantly. If he obeyed, it meant to abandon a hundred and fifty men to the enemy. If he disobeyed—

"No!" His head lifted. "I don't fear Urrea. We're too strong with men, cannon, small arms, for any force of his Mexicans. This is not the Alamo, as he'll learn. I'll not march away and leave my men to be slaughtered. I'll get off a dispatch to Ward at once, however—"

He turned back into his own quarters, preoccupied, forgetful of anything. Another officer took Desauque and Durant in hand, directing them to quarters. As they were putting up their horses, the courier voiced the thought in Durant's mind; despite the well-equipped force here, a shadow rested over the fortress mission.

"I don't like it," Desauque said simply. "I don't like that Refugio business, that silence, that choice which rends a commander asunder! I am what the Spanish call *simpatico*, and something tells me to watch out. And—I do not like that, either."

He gestured toward the flag, flattened by the breeze against

*Durant realized it was his
Mexican costume they fired at.*

the sunset-reddened sky that seemed a sea of blood. The reverse of the standard was turned, to show its second motto of "Liberty or Death." But, as they looked up at it, only the lone star and the word "Death" were visible.

Durant shrugged and remained silent. What he did not like, what he could not get out of his mind, was the look he had caught in the eyes of Fannin.

Horton's little party of cavalry came in. The sun was swallowed under the horizon. As he ate, and talked with the men around him, Durant felt the feeling of oppression vanish.

Everywhere was courage, confidence, an eagerness to meet the Mexicans face to face and avenge the Alamo.

Refugio lay twenty-five miles to the south. Even with the detachments of King and Ward gone, Fannin was left with close to three hundred men. The mystery surrounding those absent detachments was complete as though the earth had swallowed them, and swallowed the couriers sent after them, also.

Darkness had not yet fallen when Durant was abruptly summoned to Fannin's room. With the commandant was a stalwart bronzed man in the makeshift uniform of a volunteer.

The lines of worry had deepened in the face of Fannin.

"Mr. Durant," he said, "this is Captain Frazier, one of the few Texans who have joined my command. He lives at Refugio, has friends there, and knows the country. He volunteers to reach Colonel Ward, or at least to pick up information. Now, I know your story from Desauque. It's impossible for you to perform your mission to Urrea. It would be madness. That costume is of no use to you, I suggest that you turn it over to Captain Frazier—"

Durant smiled and shook his head.

"Not a bit of it, colonel. If my clothes call for special work, I refuse to lend 'em to another man. I speak Spanish; it had already occurred to me that I might ride south and pick up something. If Frazier knows the country, we might go together, one of us would reach Ward, or get back here."

"Agreed!" Frazier exclaimed. "The very thing! We can start together, then separate. I'll find friends I know of, and you can scout for news if you like. As you say, one of us should get somewhere."

S O I T was settled. Half an hour later they rode out of Goliad into the gathering darkness. Durant had left his lance behind; instead, he had pistols in his holsters, and a fresh horse.

They rode for an hour, then Frazier drew rein, pointing. The stars were thin, a gibbous moon poured ghostly radiance through misty air. Here was a trail, forking out of the main road.

"Here's hoping for the best while prepared for the worst," said the rancher. "I reckon King and Ward have both been tolled into a trap, but we can make sure. We part here, if you agree. I'm for a Mexican rancher whom I know, over near the river. He'll have sure news, and he's a friend of mine. You may scout on toward Refugio. Do we meet here—say, in two hours?"

"No," said Durant. "What use? If either of us can reach Ward, press ahead. If we find it's impossible, then get back to Goliad singly. Depends on what we learn. Fannin must have information."

"Right." Frazier gripped his hand. "*Adios*, then!"

"*Adios.*"

Durant rode on to the south, across desolate plains, through moon-filled brush, with his thoughts for company.

Doña Amadora disillusioned and in safety at San Patricio; all that was a closed book now. Faith waited in the north, the ten thousand in gold, Vincent Durant and the knife; Houston, despairing, determined, great heart in agony. Love and vengeance called out of the north. Vengeance upon that thief and destroyer, when the march of events permitted.

How long he had ridden, he did not know. His meditation was suddenly interrupted as his horse recoiled with a snort. The moon glinted feebly upon a gun barrel. A figure had upraised from the long grass and now hailed him over leveled gun.

"*Quién vive?*"

"*Amigo*," said Durant promptly. "What is it?"

"God and Liberty!" It was a ready password. A Mexican, assuredly. "Come along, friend, until I can see who you are. Is it you, Panchito?"

Durant sidled his horse in closer. "No," he responded. "I'm Miguel Vaca. And you?"

"Juan, *amigo.*"

Juan? There were a thousand Juans, but only one of import. In another moment Durant was peering down into the visage upturned to him. Eyes met eyes. A swing over saddle; then a dive, like plummet hawk striking quarry.

Durant came down headfirst, got his two hands around the man's throat as they struck earth together—got them under the musket, fingers sinking in. No time or place for pistol-shot to give alarm! The two rolled in silence, save for scuffle of brush, for thrashing feet. Durant came uppermost. The musket had been struck away.

Juan, the partner of the jaunty Jacopo—Juan, who had been sent to escort Doña Amadora to safety. He collapsed like an empty sack, in token of surrender. Durant whipped off his own scarlet sash, wrenched it asunder, and bound the man's wrists.

AFTER A moment the fellow sat up with a gasp and a groan—only to quiet at the chill of a pistol muzzle laid against his head.

"A word too loud and I'll hang your brains on the moon! You remember me, eh?"

"Assuredly, *señor*." The hapless Juan was having difficulty with his throat, but managed the hoarse croak. "You escaped, *señor?* I had nothing to do with the *ley de fuga!* It was not my doing—"

"Shut up," Durant snapped. "What are you doing here?"

"Returning, *señor*, from San Patricio."

"Where's your horse?"

"Near water, *señor*. I heard you coming and walked—"

"You lie," Durant said, and cocked the pistol. Juan shrank. "You needn't go back to camp. El Tuerto is dead, and I killed Jacopo for good measure—as I'll kill you soon enough. You wouldn't take this road back to your camp. You're alone?"

"But yes, *señor!*" bleated Juan. "My comrade stayed—"

"Another lie," struck in Durant. The man was in uniform, had doubtless joined the army of Urrea for pickings. He was on patrol duty, a sentry. There must be a picket camp near by. Thank Heaven the air was heavy, muffling voices!

"You have one chance to speak the truth—or I'll knock you on the head. Better still, blow your brains out and let your comrades come and find you." Durant stepped back a little, holding the pistol as though to fire. "Your last chance, or you'll go to hell with a lie on your lips. Are there Mexican soldiers at Refugio?"

"Yes, yes, *señor!*" broke out the fellow. "Do not kill me, for the love of God! I'll tell you everything. General Urrea is at Refugio."

"The Texans at Goliad sent down men. Where are they?"

"Part are dead, *señor*. Others got away; most are captured. That is the truth. I swear on the hilt! But I have little knowledge of what happened. Of the details."

Juan cowered. Durant hesitated, then spoke again.

"The orders? Urrea has halted at Refugio?"

"To advance, *señor*. The cavalry squadrons march before dawn to scout."

Durant caught up the remainder of the sash, and effected a gag that would serve its purpose for the moment.

"Breathe through your nose while your spittle poisons you," he rasped, and leaped for the saddle.

Goliad, now! Here was what Fannin must know. Dead, scattered, prisoners; a bad budget. Durant sent his horse back at the gallop.

He reached Goliad, made his report, flung himself down to sleep. It was broad daylight when he wakened again, refreshed at last, himself again, gauntly ready and scenting the trail ahead. Then, with afternoon, came shouts, greetings, confusion.

Frazier had just returned hellbent, running his horse to death. He had waited to get details; he had full pack.

King, given orders to retire by Colonel Ward, refused them. He and his command had been lured to a ranch outside Refugio, surrounded, captured, shot. The Georgia Battalion, under Ward, had delayed in Refugio, then had withdrawn; they had been cut off. There had been heavy firing heard. Nothing else was known; but this was enough.

"We abandon the fort and retreat to Victoria," said Fannin.

But not in a moment. Not until morning, indeed—the nineteenth of March.

THERE HAD been a little rain during the night. The morning fog, almost a drizzle, whitely cloaked the landscape. Horton's handful of cavalry had put to flight a squadron of lancers, and reported a regiment coming on the road from Bejar.

The nine cannon, to be buried by Houston's orders, were lim-
bered up; the fort, ordered blown up, was abandoned. A few
oxen tugged the heavy wagons. The cut banks of the San
Antonio River had to be leveled at the ford. It was ten o'clock
when the column passed the river and headed for Victoria,
thirty miles away. The scouts reported everything clear ahead.

"Two mistakes," muttered Captain Desauque. "Rather, three,
any one of which may prove fatal. We divided our forces and
have lost a hundred and fifty men. We've wasted time and given
Urrea a free hand. We're marching out by day in heavy order,
instead of by night in light order. The result?" He shrugged.
"*Sabe Dios!* God knows. We're not afraid, at least. Hear the men
singing?"

"A little fear might do no harm," Durant hazarded darkly.

"Bah! Americans welcome three to one! And Fannin says
Urrea won't dare halt us."

The men marched finely. A column of picked light-hearts,
enlisted for high adventure in the cause of Texas and Liberty.
All of them young, down to seventeen-year-old Hal Ripley, son
of Congressman Ripley of Louisiana. The Widow Cash, of
Goliad, rode in a wagon with her scant baggage. Her boy, fourteen, trudged in the ranks with his heritage of long rifle, powder
horn and bullet pouch. Durant looked back at the fort.

"The flag, Desauque! We've left it behind us, flying!"

"If we do not return to it. I still have that feeling about
it—you know. Well, one dies by the clock." And with this,
Captain Desauque lapsed into sombre thought.

The smothersome mist began to break. The sun flashed
through. The reefs of timber breaking through the prairie sea
became clear to the eye, serene. That heavy line of timber ahead
marked Coleto Creek, six miles away. Goliad was eight miles
to the rear. The prairie here was green, the grass thickly sprung
from a fall burn.

When the bugler orderly sounded a halt, Captain Shackleford of the Red Rovers panted up, red of face. His words were blurted out for all to hear.

"For God's sake, colonel! You're not going to halt here?"

"To rest the animals," Fannin rejoined. "They've had hard work of it."

"But they'll hold out to that timber ahead. We should keep moving; if the Mexicans come on us here, we're defenseless!" Shackleford swung on Desauque. "What do you think?"

"Naturally, I'd prefer the timber to this. But—" Desauque shrugged again. His mind had been set, his gaze reflected gloomy forebodings.

"Nonsense! We'll not be attacked," Fannin said impatiently. "We've not been followed or opposed; too late for that now. As long as our transportation doesn't break down, we're safe; our cannon and musketry would cut the enemy to pieces."

Durant flung himself down with the others for an hour's halt. Beasts grazed, men rested. From his position a few miles to the rear, Urrea had launched a thousand cavalry to the pursuit, but the signals of the cruising buzzards were unread by the column.

The march was resumed. Horton's cavalry galloped on to reconnoiter the ford of the Coleto. Slowly that heavy timber-line flanking the ford drew nearer. The going was heavy, for the ground was wet. The thin oxen were laboring again.

AN HOUR past high noon. A voice broke out somewhere, sharply. Other voices took up the burden. Eyes turned, heads swung, men twisted about. From the extended timber on the right came cantering two horsemen, with lance and pennon. Four more, to join them. Then, whole lines—cavalry by squadrons, at the trot, surging around by the right to cut off the column from the river and the timber there.

"And Horton's cavalry gone! Well, thirty men at least will reach Gonzales," said Captain Desauque with acid tongue. "We'll regret that lost hour, Durant, when we come to grips with Urrea."

The column kept moving. A six-pounder was unlimbered. Its warning roar echoed across the prairie, but the ball fell short. Now came new alarm. Four mounted scouts, posted on the back trail, came racing along, plying whip and heels.

"Run for it! We're cut off!" they yelled, as they galloped past the column. "The hull damned Mex army's a-coming!"

One of them reined in his horse and tumbled from the saddle. The other three never slackened pace, but pelted on like mad for the shelter of the timber ahead. All eyes went to the rear. Durant looked there, where the mist had broken asunder.

A glittering mass of infantry was moving rapidly, moving at the double; breaking up, deploying in the rear on the left, to surround the column. Fannin's voice rang with decision, with cheering confidence.

"March right along. Take it easy, men; don't outfoot the oxen. Those fellows can't scare us. Horton will be back and fill our hand!"

The word was passed along. The men cheered. But Horton came not back.

The enveloping movement was completed. The Mexican squadrons ahead, dismounted; at long range they made defiance with pearly bursts of musketry upon the soft air. The timber of the Coleto was but a mile onward, or a little more. The Mexicans held the trail and either flank, in force.

"If we must stand," said Desauque, "look! That rise of ground yonder. There we could hold them off until Horton and the cavalry charge them in the rear—"

Clearly, Fannin had the same thought. The march was directed for the ridge. Then the ranks faltered and shouts arose. "Wait! Hold on!" The chief ammunition wagon had broken down. The column halted. The enemy, seizing upon the moment of confusion, closed in. Desperately, Fannin ordered the column to form square—here, in the worst place to be found, this long hollow, six to ten feet below the surrounding terrain. The wagons somewhat protected the flanks.

The guns were unlimbered and began to speak.

It was the end.

Almost the end; not quite. Slowly the sun sank toward the western rim. Time after time, rolling powder-smoke burst from the hollow, white spurts joining the greater film of smoke that idly drifted in the golden air. The hours passed. Cavalry thundered down in roaring squadrons, to break and scatter and die like the powder-smoke fronting them. Infantry came on at the double, with glitter of serried bayonets, only to waver and shred apart and die.

"One hundred yards, boys—then give 'em hell!" That was Fannin, standing upright in full view among the outspread riflemen until a ball in the thigh brought him down. And the nine cannon had ceased early.

"Guns all fouled, sir," Captain Westover reported. "No water for the sponges."

Fannin smiled. "Turn your men into infantry, captain!"

THE BARED sabers, the fluttering pennons, the brave bayonets, were all scattered afar. The green prairie grass was green no longer. Bodies of men and horses strewed it thickly. The square wasted no ammunition, though the enemy's thunderous volleys were sheer futility. Half a dozen were dead, a hundred wounded—most of these from Indian bullets. A company of Campeachy redskins, sharpshooters, were strewn out along the flanks to harry the doomed square. Young Ripley had a broken hip; as the Widow Cash held him in her arms, another ball broke his arm. The shrill screams of anguished men and horses out there on the prairie were answered by groans within the square, where fevered lips implored water and found none.

"What a day!" Desauque laid down his rifle and turned to Durant. The last desperate charge had come and gone with sunset—lances and sabers and bayonets driving down into a gale of smoke and ball that scattered them afar. "What a day!

And a long night ahead. Canteens empty. No water. And no food."

"No food?" Durant repeated.

"Somebody left the provisions behind," Desauque rasped from dry throat. "A day of mistakes, eh? Well, every animal has been shot down, and we can't leave our wounded. And Horton's cavalry—ha! Wise men for you. Never came back. Damnation!" He jumped suddenly and grabbed his hat, as a ball whirred through it. "A close one, there!"

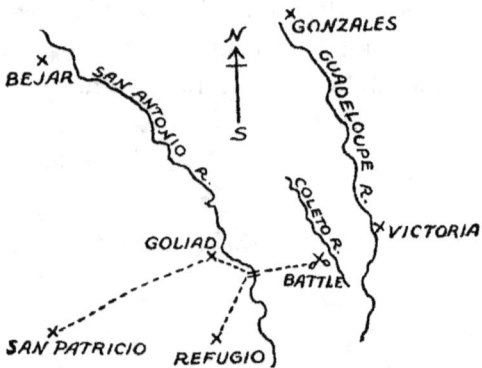

A day of mistakes, to close upon golden hearts. The dusk thickened to black fog. The clumps of tall grasses which had spurted whiffs of smoke, signaling the instant whine and thud of bullets, twinkled into fireflies. Picked men were now out, shooting back against these Indian rifles.

The golden hearts spoke. Brief conference, briefly ended. "Night and fog, the timber not far away. Those unhurt can break through. We'd have to leave the wounded."

"Leave the wounded? Be damned if we do! Stick it out!"

So decided. The weary men drew in the lines to smaller square, set to work digging a breastwork, heaping it with wagons, earth, the carcasses of animals. Durant, laboring with a spade, broke into a low mutter of cursing. There in the gloom

the pale face of young Ripley looked up at him from the arms
of the Widow Cash.

Close by, the widow's son was cleaning his long rifle ear-
nestly.

"How you feeling, soldier?" Durant demanded.

"Tol'able, sir, if I only had a drink. I downed four on 'em 'fore
I quit."

"There ain't a drop o' water in camp," the woman quavered.

"By God, there will be," said Durant, and handed his spade
to another man. He headed for Duval, captain of the Kentucky
Mustangs, on guard at this end of the square.

Duval sat beside a cannon carriage, trying to force a wiping
stick through his rifle bore. The fitful sharpshooting had ceased.
Wafted through the harsh cries for water came reiterant notes
from Mexican bugles, silvered by distance; and singsong voices
of sentinels like the utterance of night birds—"*centinela alerta!*"

Captain Duval was making hard work of it.

He held up his right hand, rudely bandaged, and grimaced.

"Some damned shave-head shot off my trigger finger—clean
as a ball! Still, I've got about five of those Injuns—laid bead on
that many pates, anyhow. Some of those snakes crawled in to
thirty yards."

Durant nodded as he chewed on a bullet to provoke saliva.

"I'm going to make a try for water, Duval—"

Noises broke suddenly. A spatter of distant musket shots, a
ripple of yells; then all was still again, ominously so. Duval
smiled grimly at his visitor.

"Someone else had the same idea, eh? No use trying to reach
the creek, Durant."

"Naturally not," said Durant, impassive, darkly contained.
"There's closer water for the having. Those Mexicans carried
canteens. There are plenty of dead ones within a hundred yards.
If I can bring in two or three canteens, they'll go a long way
with our wounded."

"That's an idea!" exclaimed Duval quickly. "You'd go alone?"

"Safest so." Durant laid aside his sombrero, and ripped the silver buttons from his jacket and pantaloons. The velvet garb was now suitable enough; smooth, noiseless, dark. "You have your men keep an eye and ear open for me—I'd hate to stop lead."

"Take a pistol, at least."

"Safer without."

"Suit yourself. Head straight out, and come straight back to this point; I'll answer for my men here. Elsewhere, fingers would be mighty light on the trigger—no one will run the chance of knife or tomahawk. Good luck, Durant!"

Slipping through the cannon opening, Durant fell flat and wormed his way forward. The black fog closed out the stars. A few Mexican picket-fires glimmered afar. The grass under him was wet.

The doomed square was swallowed up in darkness.

CHAPTER IX

MASSACRE

To DURANT the night seemed densely, impenetrably black; he had never experienced such darkness. To make cautious progress one needed the sensitive whiskers of a cat.

He was now out, how far he could not tell. There was no back view to measure distance. The entrenchments had been swallowed by the murk. The feverish plaints of the wounded were lost, the clink of tools as men labored had ceased. Thickening night and mist had doused the glimmer of the Mexican fires. Only the errant bugle calls and the admonitions of the sentries wafted occasional announcement of the enemy.

Ugh! His hand, parting the clumps of grass in exploration, plumped on something colder than the damp sod. A face cold as death, a naked body—an Indian. Durant felt about the surface of it. His hand recoiled from the shaven crown; blood, clotted icily. He tried again, found no hint of water, and wiping his hand on the grass, he crawled on.

Hereabouts the stillness was intense; the wounded had died or been carried off. He cast about for some time, edging forward to the limits of the enemy charges, when a dim mound blocked his peering eyes. His hand explored. It was a dead horse, stiff upon its side. His seeking fingers brushed a surface of cloth. The rider lay askew, pinioned by the animal, and as stiff in death. And a canteen!

Durant slipped off the straps, gripped at the canteen. Thank God it was chill and heavy, filled! He must have one drink, if only to stifle his harsh wheezing. Out here were other ears than those of the dead.

The stingy swig he allowed himself was heavenly. The temptation to take more was horrible; only the memory of those wounded, back there, held his ravening desire in check. He stoppered the canteen. Now to find a mate to it, then turn about for the camp and the parched throats awaiting him!

Then dismay whelmed him—this horse! The corner of the square, by which he had left camp, had faced only infantry charges. This canteen had come from a dragoon; therefore he had not kept a true course in the darkness. Unless he back-trailed to the post of Duval, ready to receive him, his welcome was likely to be unpleasant. As though to emphasize the thought came a muffled report from the rear, warning him of nervous fingers along the line of trench.

Well, on and get another canteen, and let the return take care of itself. And now another horse carcass. Damn the luck! What, no rider? Yet the carcass was occupied. For, as he fumbled beyond and over it, his fingers touched surface like that of a living snake, warm and rippling.

His wrist was gripped fast and jerked forward. The rank odor of an Indian tingled his nostrils. A face was pressed almost against his.

"*Quién vive?*"

"*Amigo!*" gasped Durant, instantly realizing what had happened. "And you, *hombre?*"

"Campeachy."

The grunted word brought no relaxation of the grip. Durant gathered himself to pounce, to grapple. He caught a sudden startled exclamation—his fist drove forward and smashed into the visage fronting him. The grip relaxed.

But, at this instant, a movement from behind; a heavy form crushed Durant flat. A hand gripped over nose and mouth. A second Indian there! The first was in upon them now. Durant

was overborne, half suffocated, throttled. A club smashed
against his head, and again, stunning him.

ONLY FOR a moment; but he wakened to find arms and
ankles bound fast as he lay beside the dead horse. Even this
slight scuffle had roused the Texans. Panicky shouts arose. Rifles
cracked. A number of Indians were squatting around him with
clicking tongues. They reached decision. Two of them hoisted
Durant by legs and shoulders and started off with him, unboth-
ered by the murk, by the black terrain. Now and again they set
him down; one of them broadly sat upon him while they
grunted and rested.

Voices rose in the darkness and grew nearer. The flames of a
small fire grew upon a background of trees, touching several
standing figures there, alert and listening. One of the Indians
spoke out; the response was quick and urgent.

"*Quién vive?*"

"Campeachy."

"Come on, then."

The two Indians, with Durant slung between them, made in
past the picket post, and entering the circle of firelight, dumped
their burden there.

"*Caramba!* A live man!"

Rapid colloquy followed, with one of the Indians speaking
broken Spanish. Durant caught a significant word: *espia*—spy!
Soldiers brusquely kicked him up. His feet were freed. Led by
a slip-noose about his neck and prodded by a bayonet, he was
conducted on again, emerging at last from darkness.

"The prisoner, my general."

Durant was left standing alone. The tent was lighted by a
guttering candle whose flame rose without a quaver in the
breathless air. General Urrea, a bushy man, sat upon a camp cot
in slippers and negligée. A black and red serape folded about
him kept out the chill of the March night. He plucked at his
raven imperial and thoughtfully stared at the prisoner.

"You were taken as a spy, I am told. Do you speak Spanish?"

"A spy? Assuredly not, *señor*."

Durant's voice was more confident than his heart. Recognition again as Vincent Durant? Unlikely. But, whether charged on his own account or on that of Vincent, he stood upon very thin ice.

"Your name?"

"Gordon. I am no spy, *señor*. I was taken outside your lines and brought in."

"True. Yet you're from the camp of the Texan rebels," barked Urrea. "You were caught creeping toward our lines. You're in Mexican costume; to be less remarked, you stripped the buttons from it. You speak Spanish. What were you doing, then?"

Durant stood silent for an instant. Then:

"Deserting," he said calmly. The black brows of Urrea arched.

"So? Then as a coward you deserve death; on all counts, in fact. The rebels have no water? They are in desperate straits?"

"Not at all." Durant spoke with cool assurance. "The wagons are loaded with water. General Houston and two thousand men are marching to join us. In all the fighting today we had only six men killed."

Urrea scowled briefly, with a certain wonder, then broke into a laugh

"Come! I retreat; you are not a coward. Therefore you're a spy. You were no doubt foraging for canteens of water when my Indians caught you. No, no, *hombre*; we know too much to be taken in by your fine words! Your cavalry have vanished. Your Houston is on the march, but not in this direction. He and your rebel government are in wild flight, tails between their legs, for safety. As for you—well, you know the fate of a spy, rebel or no. Have you anything to say before I order you shot?"

DURANT SHRUGGED lightly, then stood impassive.

"Yet I am merciful, and you are a brave *hombre*," said Urrea thoughtfully. "I spare your life, on one condition. Return to your camp. Inform Colonel Fannin that I have five thousand troops here, and am expecting three thousand more with morning. That, if he surrenders at daylight, I offer him terms. Otherwise, he receives no quarter. I'll have you taken through my camp to see for yourself, that you may the better advise him. Do you agree?"

Life, and an open trail to Vincent, Faith, other duty! At no great price. Or he might lie to this man, tell Fannin the truth. Small good it would do, any of it. A revulsion of feeling swept Durant—a sudden gusty impatience of lies, trickery, false pretenses of any kind. To hell with all that!

"The Texans have sufficient ammunition, and patience, to kill your whole five thousand men, my general," he rejoined. "That is, when you get them. My thanks; your offer is refused."

"*Muy bien*," Urrea uttered carelessly, and leaned back. "So much the worse for you. A true *caballero*, eh?"

He fingered his mustache, his black imperial. His hand dropped to the edge of the cot, fingers drumming a quickstep there as he stared at Durant, reflectively. The guttering candle flickered in a stealthy draught until it animated derisive shadows which advanced and retreated. The officer and guards at the tent entrance stood motionless.

"You are bold, you play a part, you speak Spanish," said Urrea slowly. "There has been such a man at large—hm! A dispatch from His Excellency—the strange tale of Doña de la Vega— hm! My secretary will have the details. Hm! I shall need an interpreter in the morning to confer with your rebel friends. Do you give me your word to speak the truth? If so, I'll remand you as a prisoner for further investigation."

A straw at which to catch with clean hands.

"As interpreter? You have my word of honor, my general," said Durant promptly.

He was marched away under close guard.

He rested ill that night; the future seemed darker than the starless murk itself. Leg irons and a special guard. What chance here to evade? None, at the moment. He had grasped at the future; he must await it, take what might turn up, watch each instant.

Dawn swept through the camp with silvery blare of bugle, excited voices, rumbling of wheels and clatter of caisson; artillery had come up, and fresh squadrons. Daylight roared down the prairie with scourging rounds of grape and canister. It was met by a desperate and deadly response from outraged rifles.

Then the white flag.

Durant was taken forward with Colonel Salas, a German officer named Holzinger, and another. To meet them came Colonel Fannin, hobbling on makeshift crutches, with Major Ben Wallace and Captain Desauque. They gave Durant swift recognition, heard that neither of the Mexican officers spoke English, understood his position. Fannin's words were clear.

"WELL, I have no water; my wounded need attention. I particularly recommend these unfortunates to you. I'll surrender at the discretion of the Mexican government—"

"No, no, colonel!" broke in Desauque in swift alarm. He flung Durant an appealing glance, a frantic appeal to keep silence. Durant nodded. "Let me translate. You mean, on the proper terms." He turned to Colonel Salas. "Colonel Fannin will surrender his force upon promise that he and they will be granted the terms customary for prisoners of war among civilized nations."

"You are a Mexican, sir?" asked Salas.

"No, my colonel. French, of New Orleans; now of Texas."

Colonel Salas frowned. "I have no authority to make terms. I'm appointed to receive his capitulation under the white flag. If you'll write down the conditions I'll submit them to General Urrea—final approval, however, rests with the supreme command."

Fannin, in great pain from his wound, flushed at hearing this.

"We've no writing materials here, Desauque; wait here until

I return and get the conditions written out. They should provide for the respect of private property; proper treatment; the men to be returned to the United States, the officers paroled for the same destination. I'll prepare the articles."

He hobbled away, with Major Wallace. Desauque moved over to Durant.

"So you were captured, eh? We supposed as much."

"By the Indians, yes."

"Well, we're in for it," said Desauque moodily. "We should have fought it out. Fannin was willing; the majority voted us down. The Alamo—that was on a Sunday. Today is Sunday; Passion Sunday, I believe. There'll be another Sunday. Confound it! The calendar has too many Sundays."

Durant laughed, though he recalled the words later.

"Nonsense! The terms will be granted."

"By whom? Now we're told that we're not dealing with Urrea, but with Santa Anna."

Holzinger caught the names, came over and joined them, with stiff Spanish speech.

"Gentlemen? You must understand; the final decision rests with the President. But General Urrea is an honorable man. I'm confident that in ten days it will be liberty and home for you all. We're close to the Gulf ports, where there are ships."

Desauque shrugged, with sardonic mien.

So the articles were drawn up, signed, approved. The column of prisoners was marched back to Goliad. So, also, was Durant. Once there, his irons were knocked off and he was turned into the mission church with the others.

Two hundred of them, crowded, packed, jammed in here. The wounded, of both sides, were stuffed into the small hospital of the Mexican barracks. Rations, four ounces of saltless jerked beef per day, to each man. After the first day, rested, refreshed, the despondent hearts began to swell in exultation. Home lay ahead, a return was promised quickly.

"The damned deserter! You, mister, keep to yourself. We need all the fresh air we can get in this hogpen."

So came to a head the black looks of a little group about Durant's corner, as he heard himself addressed. The speaker was a tall Alabaman named Sinton.

"Duval says he went out after water," spoke up someone.

"Yes, and never came back; took information to the enemy. Then they knew they had us thirsted out." The unkempt, grimy Alabaman, rasped to the raw by discomfort and hunger, glowered at Durant, who remained silent, impassive.

"Well, we've got good terms, haven't we?"

"No thanks to him," rasped Sinton. The man was venomous, unreasonable. "And how do we know we got good terms?"

"Fannin says so; everybody knows it. Aw, shucks! Think about home, Sinton. We're headed for home, you big galoot!"

A FEW others felt as Sinton did about Durant; said no word. He was not one to argue, to appeal, to explain. The game here was finished; he was thinking again about Vincent, about the trail that led—whither? No telling, now.

Rumor, gossip, news, seeped through. Ships were at the coast, being made ready to take them to New Orleans. All Texas was in mad flight for the Louisiana border. Gonzales had been burned, Santa Anna was sweeping the country with fire and sword. The government was gone on the run. Houston had no men and had disappeared. The Texan army had simply evaporated.

Then, one night, came slogging feet and despondent men, stuffing every nook and corner of the old mission church. Colonel Ward and eighty-five of his Georgia Battalion, all left alive, as bagged in the swamps of the Guadeloupe; not a pleasant reunion.

Hard on their heels, eighty more men—strangers, this time. Major Miller and his Tennessee volunteers from Nashville, come to join the Texan cause, and grabbed as they came ashore at the Gulf. For some mysterious reason, Urrea had ordered a

strip of white cloth tied about an arm of each of these Tennes-
seeans; they were warned not to remove the badge. They were
bantered right and left about their "white flags."

"Why?" Captain Desauque shrugged when Durant questioned him. His eyes rested on the white badges moodily. "How
should I know? Well, I have an idea; but it's fantastic. No, never
mind."

Saturday saw Fannin back from a painful trip down to the
coast, with report that no ships were at hand, but within a few
days would be available. There was singing that night. One of
the men had a flute. The strains of "Home Sweet Home" roared
among the church rafters. Guards gathered under the windows
to listen. Mexican women peered in. Their round faces, shroud-
ed in black mantillas, were soft with compassion. The men
waved cheerily and sang their lustiest. Another few days had
passed. Tomorrow was Sunday—Palm Sunday. Time had quick-
ened. Soon a ship, two ships—then home!

"I've come for the American named Gordon."

A sergeant and a squad of soldiers came in at the front door.
His peremptory demand silenced the music, stilled the voices.
Durant sat against the wall, talking with Captain Desauque.
The latter turned, acting swiftly, tearing the white rag from the
arm of the nearest Tennesseean and binding it about Durant's
sleeve.

"Say nothing! We never heard of you," muttered Desauque.

"By command of the general!" blared out the sergeant angrily.
"El hombre Gordon! The spy, the man in our camp. Where is
he?"

The tall Alabaman, Sinton, leaped up.

"Thar he is, the hound!" he cried, pointing. "Take him and
good riddance!"

"Shame, shame!" rose indignant, generous voices. But Durant
flung the false badge from his arm, came to his feet, and made
his way through the massed throngs.

"I'm the man you want. What is it?"

"Step forward; you will come with me," the sergeant replied. He added: "Say goodby if you like. You'll not be back."

A hearty grip from Desauque, other hands extended cordially, voices bidding farewell; few joined in the suspicions of the Alabaman. The squad of men closed about Durant and led him outside, and halted again.

"Your pardon," the sergeant said. "You're a large man. You're to be tied, and tightly. Arms behind you!"

DURANT WAS bent forward. Thongs were laid upon wrists and arms until the flesh screamed. Durant submitted.

"Whither are you taking me?"

"To Colonel Portilla, at the camp yonder. You're to be held *incommunicado.*"

They started for the camp. The atmosphere of the place was strangely quiet, for a Saturday night—a quiet heavy with protest and foreboding, a quiet of tensed nerves. The soldiers moved on aimless feet or squatted in groups of furtive gossip. The mirth of the cantina where liquor flowed was subdued. A priest shuffled along with head bowed.

Abruptly a woman blocked the way. She wore black, and by face and carriage was a matron. Her face, framed in lacy mantilla, was troubled, with sensitive lips compressed. Durant felt her gaze envelop him like that of a mother.

"What's this, sergeant? A prisoner?" A woman of rank, evidently. Her voice was one of authority. The sergeant saluted her.

"Yes, *señora.* One of the Americans. To Colonel Portilla."

Durant heard her murmur: "*Pobrecito!* Poor fellow!" Then she spoke impulsively, angrily.

"But he is cruelly tied! Why, those cords cut into his arms, they bend him over, his hands are purple and swollen—this is inhuman, sergeant! You do not fear one man? Loosen him."

"Those are the orders, *señora,*" the sergeant stammered. "He is said to be a most desperate man—"

"I am Señora Alvarez, wife of Captain Alvarez of the army,"

she broke in firmly. "It was I who aided the comfort of those Americans who were lately brought in. General Urrea approved when I caused them to be untied, to be treated like human creatures. Loose this man, sergeant! I will be responsible. Why, you're nine men, with muskets—and you torture him? Brave men can be generous. At least, tie him less tightly."

The sergeant scratched his head.

"Well, well, *señora*, perhaps I made the cords too tight. I'll take them off, let the blood circulate, then tie him more loosely. After all, we are nine; that is true. And the responsibility is to you."

The sergeant fell to work. The squad lounged at ease; the *señora* looked on, her hands clasped, her lips moving. Durant caught her murmurs.

"I can do no more, no more. And all those others—may tomorrow never come!"

What did she mean? Well, what of it? For a blessed moment the blood surged into his aching hands. Be tied again—be led like a sheep to the slaughter?

Durant burst into action. The river, darkly fringed with trees, whispered him "Now or perhaps never!" To a stout kick the sergeant went sprawling. The group of soldiers swirled and broke before impact of fists and body. Then Durant was running full tilt for the river and the line of timber.

Shouts arose, of command, of alarm. Muskets began to crash; lead whistled around, but not close. Dim light, poor marksmen. Now it was a chase—let them catch him if they could!

Tongues of flame jetted from the gathering darkness. Shadows converged; patrols, an outpost charging in to head him from the river. Durant ran grimly, every sense alert, every muscle poised and ready. A burly form and grinning face came squarely into his path. The soldier lunged forward with the bayonet; the wavering steel missed as Durant swerved, but the man was quick to recover and he swung in with the butt. Durant took the blow, kicked out, caught the musket and wrenched it

free. He drove home the bayonet, and tried to jerk it clear; the
steel was too tightly housed. He left musket and man, pushing
on while shouts and whistling balls pursued him.

THE DANK breath of the river touched his dry nostrils.
He came to the cut bank, hesitated not, went head first into
the black water. The cool depths enfolded him like a benediction
of peace after pain. Fortune had guided him. The current here
swept strong, it was deep in flood with the rains to the north.

Even in the act he had kept his head. Even in the dive he
switched about and reversed direction. Half by guess, half by
instinct, he broke surface right against the bank from which he
had leaped. They would not look for him here of all places.

Right! Quick wits saved him there. The earth shook to the
thud of hastening feet. Voices sounded directly above him in
curse, threat, command. Muskets flared. Up and down stream
the water was gashed by smacking lead as the shots challenged
moving objects, seen or fancied.

The bank overhung him here. He stayed rooted, in mud and
water to his waist. The ardor of pursuit lapsed. Voices told him
everything. "If he got across, they'll pick him up on the other
side." "The river swallowed him." "My ball split his head, I tell
you!" "He never came up. That belly-flop knocked the wind out
of him."

Durant waited, a long while, for certainty. The opposite shore
held peril; no haven of safety there. He peeled off his garments;
then, with heart exultant and body lightened, he launched
himself out into the current and let it take him. Sullen, aboil
with mud, the heavy water tugged at him, bore him along as
he swam. On down stream and on, gradually coming across to
the farther bank in the darkness. The fringe of bushes received
him, He gained footing and staggered for the shore, to sink
down in close covert and lie panting, shivering, triumphant,
grim thanks to Señora Alvarez of the pitying heart.

Gradually the shivers passed. Drowsy, he planned to stay
where he was until daylight. He had doffed his boots with the

rest. A naked man would have small joy of the chaparral at night, and make small headway. Morning would tell him what he needed to know of pursuit, of situation. He fell asleep on the thought, well content.

Muscles stiff, he lurched up in the gray dawn, every sense alert. He had been carried by the stream halfway to the ford below town. Bugles shrilled, the little clanking church bells were sounding. Early mass of Palm Sunday? The Devil's mass, rather.

The measured tread of marching men, the sound of voices, drew him. He hunted loophole in the growth of brush and trees. A double file of infantry enclosed a double file of Texans, prisoners from the church precincts, Desauque heading them. Dragoons closed the rear. Foot and horse marched steadily, as with a purpose, down this road to the lower ford. Yonder, above the town, another similar procession was emerging upon the road to San Antonio, in the northwest; a third procession was forming up at the church.

Removal of prisoners—for better quarters, for exchange, for home? Not so. The column had halted. Durant, watching, saw the prisoners gathering brush. They were well, they were talking and laughing as the piles of brush grew into heaps. Then, against the heaps, he saw them formed up in line. He watched, puzzled.

AT THIS moment, back in Goliad, Colonel Fannin was being aided out to a stone bench and seated upon it. The wounded were being carried out. The eyes of Fannin dwelt upon the file of soldiers facing him, dwelt coolly, calmly, bravely. He alone of them all, knew the truth—he alone had been told of the orders from Santa Anna.

"Don't shoot me in the face—that's all I ask," he said quietly.

But Durant, watching his comrades lined up before the brush-heap, had no inkling. He saw the squads of infantry lining up. The Texans faced the brush-heap. Behind them, the infantry muskets swung to shoulder. The officer's sword was uplifted in command. One of the Texans looked around.

"My God, boys!" His voice lifted shrill on the morning. "They're going to kill us—"

The sword flashed in downward arc. The muskets gushed smoke; the jarring volley rolled and rolled. The smoke thinned. Men were down, flat, huddled, creeping in a welter of dead and dying. A few knelt. Others swung around to face death. Some broke and ran for the river.

They scattered, ran hellbent for the river and timber. Durant's eyes gripped to one, a tall, rawboned figure in volunteer's rig, who ran with prodigious leaps and bounds like a hunted buck. A Mexican soldier, outfooted, halted and threw up his piece, and the shot gushed. The fugitive stumbled, recovered, leaped on again. A dragoon came after him at the gallop. With a frantic leap the fugitive went into air and landed in the river, spread-eagled. The dragoon reined in, snatched out pistol, waited. The head came up. The pistol bellowed, and the head vanished. After a moment the dragoon, satisfied, wheeled his horse and went back to the slaughter.

Durant made haste; he alone had understood, had seen. He ran to help the man who had swum under water, who now came crawling out through the shallows. Durant caught him, helped him on into the screening timber.

Bolstered against a tree, the haggard face of the Alabaman contorted.

"So it's you. No use, pardner; streak it while you can."

"Shut up," snapped Durant, busy. "Let me get this hole bandaged—"

"Nope, I'm a goner," said Sinton. "Mister, will you shake hands? I played you a skunk trick. Duval and the others set me right."

Durant took the cold hand in his. "Never mind; you did me a good turn, perhaps, by pointing me out. Now let me clap these rags over the wound—"

No use; the man was slipping fast. His eyes wearily yielded to the drooping lids. Life was on the flutter.

"They told us—we were going home," he muttered. "To a ship. Damned snakes! They give us our ticket all right. You tell my mammy—I—"

The head jerked forward. The lips set in a fixed smile.

The killers were busy looting and stripping the dead, flinging the bodies upon the piles of brush, and firing the brush. The dragoon horses took fright at the gushing smoke and flames of the pyre; they broke loose, dashed about, came wandering every way. Their riders, arguing and fighting over loot, paid no heed at the moment.

But Durant, catching one of the loose horses, sought not only to live. By day, by night, by prairie and timber, he rode to vengeance. Nose to trail, hand to knife—dark, naked as any Indian, careless of thirst or hunger—he rode.

CHAPTER X

DISASTER AHEAD

DURANT CAME to El Encinal del Perdido, The Live-oak Wood of the Lost, as the Mexicans well styled the battlefield of the Coleto. Here he picked up a serape, odds and ends of clothes. Already he had rations in the saddle pockets of his horse, and a pair of roweled spurs from dead feet sent him on his way serene.

Gonzales? He must try Gonzales, of course. No further word from the north had filtered through to Goliad, though the Mexicans had declared that Houston's army and all the countryside were in wild flight. Here in the south there was evidence of this flight. San Patricio, Refugio, Goliad, had been emptied of settlers' families, whose goal was the Trinity River in the east. Beyond this, again, lay the Sabine; and still farther lay the Louisiana frontier of the United States. Thus, in constantly increasing stream, went the rout from the land of Texas, a land condemned to death and ruin by the invader.

Durant struck for Gonzales, where he had left Faith. That Vincent had gone there, was certain. There, by hook or by crook, he would pick up some news of them. Gonzales was the junction where the trails would fork.

He was cautious, unhasty, dogged now as for months past, pressing forward with a terrible patience to his one aim.

Firelight radiance warned him afar; it was of an evening that he neared Gonzales. Abandoning the road, he swam his horse across the Guadeloupe to the eastern bank, below where stood the town, and foraged onward carefully. On his course north he had met no living soul. Now he realized there was none here to greet him.

Across the stream by the ford, the camp-fires of a Mexican bivouac twinkled. Clink of equipment and the chatter of voices reached across, in the lowering mist. But never a light in Gonzales. Only the blackened skeleton of a town was here, its ashes long cold and dead.

Faith was gone, old man Hittel, Vincent, Houston, settlers, army—gone. None of the Mexicans were on this side, for at the moment the river was rushing high with the influx of heavy rains and crossing was difficult. Durant wandered unchallenged in the darkness.

He sought and discovered the camp site of those Texan volunteers, once rallied here to await the decision of the Alamo. Here had stood Sam Houston's tent, where for a brief moment he had looked upon Faith Hittel's face again, where he had met Desauque, where he had been lifted by Houston into the tide of events, of courage and of pitiful horror. Farther on was a charred mount of baggage and supplies, hastily destroyed by fire before the Mexican advance.

All gone; the whole place now tenanted only by voiceless phantoms, by the ashes of domestic hearths and martial camp-fires. The Mexican vaunt had not been mere bombast. The country here, as in the south, had been abandoned in panic and confusion. And how far did it go, this retreat?

The dawn trail pointed eastward. Two trails, rather, diverging; Durant, reins over arm, read the sign with glittering eyes as he followed. One trail, the fresher of the two, indicated a solid column of horse, foot and artillery; Mexicans, then, had passed this way.

THE OTHER trail, a little northward, showed loosely marching men, wagon tire and ox hoof, women's feet, and could be marked by household goods jettisoned in the mud. Here was the trail of panic and despair, to be followed in calmness and

It was old Hittel!

in hope. Here went Houston and Faith—God grant!—and the crafty old man her father. And this trail might well branch into another that would point to Vincent and the gold. Durant smiled with grim lips, and reached for the saddle.

The Mexican reveille from across the river was wafted faintly to his ears. He rode on all the day through a land of prairie and of post-oak islands, with never a stir of human life. He came upon settlers' cabins, deserted, their fugitives broadening this trail of flight. The army, the horde rather, had camped, had pillaged fences and trees for firewood, had gone on. The story was written in the earth.

Next day he came up to a cabin he deemed equally empty, but it was not. A white-bearded man sat on a bench beside the shack entrance, a horse pistol across his high knees, a dribble of tobacco juice bestrewing his beard. When Durant saw him and drew rein, he vented quavering welcome.

"Howdy, stranger! Light and tie, or be you on the run, too? If you're one o' them Mexican varmints I warn ye I ain't to be skeered and I've nary word to give ye."

"No Mexican, and not running," said Durant. "I'm trying to catch up with the army ahead. How far on is Houston?"

"The hull passel of 'em passed by two weeks back," responded the veteran. "They were bound for Burnham's Crossin' down on the Colorado. I heered tell Sam Houston was calculatin' to make a stand at the Colorado, but there was a column o' Mexicans racing him to the south. Most like, when he l'arned of 'em he changed his mind. The men said he'd promised he'd fort in the tall timber east o' Gonzales and fight from there, but he kep' on going. Mebbe he's still a-going."

"And you didn't join the march?"

"Me? No!" The veteran spat hugely. "I ain't too old to fight, but I'm too old to run. I fit in the Revolution and I fit agin at sixty under Gin'ral Jackson at New Orleens. I've put in a crop here, and here I set. Everybody else skedaddled. If ary o' them yaller varmint come nigh enough I'll gin 'em Jackson and New Orleens!"

"I s'pose you don't happen to know old man Hittel of Gonzales?" Durant asked at a venture, as he stretched his legs.

"Sure I do. Seed him, too. He drapped by long enough for a drink."

"Was his daughter with him?"

"Huh? A gal? I disremember. Hold on, stranger! Seems like he mentioned—yes, he did. Said he'd sent her ahead to San Felipe, east o' the Colorado. He reckoned she'd be safe yonder."

With hasty farewell, Durant mounted and rode on into the east, leaving white-beard, horse pistol in lap, to defy the "yaller varmints."

At long last, the Colorado river showed ahead, full sixty miles from Gonzales.

Durant swam the swollen river, finding the crossing silent and deserted; and so was Burnham's settlement beyond. The buildings had been burned. The trail of refugees led on eastward, as though the country hereabouts were all abandoned like the region to the west.

The main trail, that of the army, led down along the east side of the river, fifteen miles, to Beason's on the lower ford. Durant went warily, descrying smoke from afar. Here in the cleared timber close to Beason's settlement, he gazed across the river; campfires, uniforms red and blue, mounted patrols, the murmur of many voices, the distant clink and clatter of tools above the rushing waters. The Mexican column was there, and waiting to cross. The river, at full flood, was a barrier and safeguard.

ALTHOUGH DURANT had long since lost all count of time, it was the fifth of April. Santa Anna was hard behind his advance column.

On, in the drizzling dawn, cutting through the river bend. The trail pointed into east once more, a trail of retreat and rout. By the signs, however, he was now closing in upon the flight.

The Brazos River and San Felipe were thirty miles away—nearer forty, by a trail of rain and mud. Faith would be there, sheltered, with her crafty father. Houston and the army would be there, faced about at last, to hold the line of the Brazos. The heavy rains, swelling all the streams to flood stage, would delay the Mexican artillery and blunt the thrusted lance-columns spreading over Texas. The retreat surely had some plan. Reinforcements must have gathered. The Brazos would become the Rubicon of Texan freedom.

On and on led the desolate, empty trail, to end in black dismay.

San Felipe de Austin—the first capital, the town of aristocrats, of wealthy settlers, of fine homes, the cradle of Western liberty! Durant reined in, staring, incredulous, dumb with bitter disappointment. Burned, abandoned, trees and houses a blackened fire-waste. No Faith here. No Houston. No army. A hundred miles of frontier, of settlements and farms, all abandoned to the invader—and now this!

Suddenly a figure appeared, sidling his horse forward from concealment, his long rifle advanced and ready. A familiar shape, this. Durant found himself returning the anxious, peering gaze of Deef Smith, last seen in Houston's tent, now here met again in the ruins beside the Brazos. The rain was falling coldly from a gray, dismal sky.

"Know you," croaked Deef. "Back agin, huh? Where from?"

"Goliad, by way of Gonzales," Durant responded.

"What say?" Deef's hand went to his ear. "Goliad? News?"

"All dead."

"Huh? Heard Fannin surrendered."

"He did. A week later the men were marched out and shot. I got away, but saw it happen. Don't know about Fannin. Desauque was killed, and the others."

"Huh? You lying? Shot—for what? How many?"

"Every man, I reckon. Marched out on the prairie, lined up, shot down."

The seamed, leathery countenance of Deef Smith was twisted by a spasm of such savage fury that the sweat beaded his dark brow. A torrent of low, tense oaths poured from his lips, then was checked. The convulsive surge of emotion died; the red glare in his eyes cooled, and he was the wary Indian again.

"There'll be reckoning," he said hoarsely. "Where bound?"

"For Houston. Where is he?"

"Up river eighteen mile in the Brazos bottoms—at Groce's Crossin'. Camped."

"Seen anything of Faith Hittel? Or her father?"

"Dunno. Most o' them settlers have kep' a-going. Seen any Mex?"

"There's a column camped in the post-oaks on the west side of the river, above Beason's."

Hand cupping ear, Deef Smith nodded.

"Gin'ral Woll and Sesma; eight hundred. We left 'em there. Was all set to fight. Had fourteen hundred; looked like fight sure. The gin'ral backed and filled. Halfbreed name o' Kerr come in, give news o' Fannin's bust-up. Half the army lit out to protect their fam'lies. Hell bust loose. Santy Anna was comin' and panic everywhere. No show for a fight. Had to back up."

IT WAS a lengthy speech for Deef Smith; evidently he was much exercised. He paused for breath, then queried: "Know anything about Santy Anna?"

Durant shook his head. "No. There were troops across from Gonzales, though."

"Three columns in drive—south, middle, north," clucked Deef Smith. "Middle 'un chasing us. Ketch Santy Anna, got all Mexico. He's allus in a hurry. Likely with middle column. Our meat." Deef Smith drew breath, "I'm on the scout. Me, Handy, Karnes. Hell of a job, this weather, can't see or hear well. Swim your hoss over. Cap'n Mose Baker's company's guarding the crossin', east end—hello! Here's Baker now. I'll scout back trail. Mebbe pick up a greaser—"

Deef Smith rode on. A different sort of speech from Captain Moseley Baker of the San Felipe volunteers.

"Sam Houston? To hell with him! We're done retreating. If we follow that old fox he'll take us to cover clear at Nacogdoches where he could duck for the United States and leave our country to the Mexicans. I know where he's heading for, and he knows that I know, and a lot more with me. Two companies here, mine and Martin's; we've quit him. He went up to Groce's Crossing without us. Why he went I don't know. The boys are aiming to elect another commander."

Baker stormed oaths lustily. "If we'd had a fighting man instead of an old woman over us, nary a Mex would ha' crossed the Guadeloupe back yonder, and nary a family needed to leave their homes this side the Guadeloupe. We had rising of four hundred as good men as ever sighted a rifle, including Sherman's Kentucky Volunteers, and Sesma was coming for us from Bejar with only seven hundred. Huh! What happened? We left Fannin holed up at Goliad, abandoned the Guadeloupe, abandoned the Colorado, and now the Brazos is lost. I'm put to guarding this crossing with only forty men. And Houston has taken himself and the heft of the army upriver. Why? He aims to cross there and go on to the Louisiana border. And now the Brazos settlers are joining the mob and running. The government has high-tailed out o' Washington, up-river. All hands running! Fannin and his men surrendered, I hear."

"Murdered," said Durant.

Men came running. Shouts, yells, oaths of ferocity filled the air when the tale of Goliad was known. Baker and his men went wild with savage intensity of passion. Then, after a time, Baker heard the questions Durant was repeating at him.

"Old man Hittel of Gonzales? Settler?" he rasped. "Seems to me there was some poor old devil looking for his gal. No gal of his in San Felipe. I burned it myself, after seeing the folks out. The gal may have gone on to Washington—hear they're clearing out o' there, too. You'll likely get word of Hittel when you catch up with Houston—"

Looking for his gal? Durant rode on, spurred upriver, sudden frantic dismay in his heart.

The skies had cleared. The waning afternoon promised a fair sunset, when Durant rode through the swampy Brazos bottoms west of the river, opposite Groce's plantation, there to find Houston and the army of Texas. It was not Houston, nor the sentinels, who halted him, however.

"Ye damned lying scoundrel!" went up a wild, shrill yell of fury. "What've you done with my gal?"

Durant drew rein, staring at the horrible, avenging figure that confronted him.

CHAPTER XI

RETREAT

OLD HITTEL tottered forward, seized the bridle curb in gnarled, trembling fist, and forced the horse to its haunches.

"What've you done with my gal?" he leveled accusing demand. "Speak up!"

"Easy; let go my bridle," Durant cautioned. "Faith? I've done nothing with her. I came here to find her. How is it you don't know where she is? Quick, man!"

The old man bawled out an oath. He was ragged, muddy, bearded and grisly, wrinkled face quivering and faded blue eyes hotly watering.

"You've done nothing with her? Damn you! When I gin her over to ye to be put safe—her and that store o' money!" His fist rose, charged with wrath. "What've you done with her? Where's the money? Speak up, afore I kill ye!"

Durant dismounted, glanced around, and beckoned to a fallen tree.

"Come on; sit down, Hittel. There's a big mistake here some-where. Just who do you think I am?"

"Gordon Durant, blast ye! I know ye well enough. Don't deny it, do ye?"

"No," Durant replied calmly. Already his sinking heart had foreseen the truth. "But you never gave Faith over to me. I've not seen you since New Orleans."

"What?" blazed out the old man. "You didn't come to my

house in Gonzales after dark, nigh three weeks back, an' ride off with my gal and that store o' money for San Felipe, ag'in time I could foller?"

"I never saw your house in Gonzales." Durant regarded him steadily. Indian features impassive, dark eyes aglitter with anxiety and yet for the moment composed. The truth he must have at once. He could only get it by explanation.

"I've told you, in past days, of my half-brother Vincent. I came to Gonzales and Faith took me to be Vincent; I was in Mexican uniform. This was in Houston's tent. The general himself knows the truth. Later, after I'd been forced to ride away without a word to you or her, Vincent showed up. Evidently she took him for me. After dark, eh? Yes, he could get away with it then. The same thing, in New Orleans; after dark. Look closely, Hittel! Am I the man who came to your house?"

Hittel leaned forward, squinting as he focused the rheumy eyes of age.

"I sw'ar! It beats me," he said doubtfully. "Yes, Faith mentioned Vincent bein' in company wi' that Spanish woman. We knowed he was at Bejar. Afterwards, next day, Houston allowed it was you all the time. Now I look close—yep, I see a difference." He leaned back, puckered and shaken, and wiped his eyes.

"Then 'twarn't you who took Faith."

"Tell me," Durant prompted. "Speak quickly. What happened?"

"Why, Gawd rot him, he come along after nightfall. Said he'd been turned back, couldn't git through to wherever he'd been sent. We was all in a pother there. What with the massacree at the Alamo, and Santy Anny on the way, I tell you it was a panic! He didn't let on he warn't you. He even had your papers and knife—"

"He jumped me and took everything from me," Durant said.

"You don't say! Well, he talked us fair enough. Ye see, Houston had spoke to us, and it guaranteed him. It was candle-light and warn't much time; everybody in a stew to git off or git caught by Santy Anny. I told him to take Faith and that thar gold—"

"The ten thousand dollars you stole from the Mexican woman, eh?"

HITTEL GAVE him a sharply defiant look, old face working with anger.

"Stole? Not me. You know about it, huh? Well, I opened that Mexican chest; me and Deef Smith together. Jewels and such like, she said, but it warn't. Gold! Mexican gold, too. Spoil of the 'Gyptians, I says, when I seed it. Deef Smith wouldn't take none. I'm a pore man. If I had to be druv away from what I had, Faith and me might have something yet; so I took it. Fair enough!"

"Never mind. Where's Faith?"

"I gin her and the money to the feller I thought was you. He was to take 'em to San Felipe, light out ahead o' me, 'cause I had to pack up 'fore gitting off. But I ain't had word of 'em, ain't seen hide nor hair of man or gold or gal. My ox team bruk down and when I got to San Felipe it was bein' burned."

"All right, we'll find her," Durant said, words more confident than heart. "She couldn't have stayed long with Vincent; she'd discover the cheat. Houston must have told her enough to warn her against such mistakes. She may have gone to Washington, on the Brazos."

"Mebbe. You find her and that gold," Hittel implored brokenly, greed marked in his clutching fingers. "I'll share it with ye. It's yourn and Faith's, anyhow. I been up to Washington myself. Nobody there. Hull gover'ment lit a shuck. Gone to Harrisburg on Buffler Bayou, down near Galveston Bay. The settlers all skipped hellhound for acrost the Trinity. By Gawd," and the old man sobbed a wild curse, "think of us Americans takin' to the woods for a pack o' Mexicans, and our gin'ral running ahead! If it hadn't been for Faith and that money, I'd ha' stayed with old Daddy Spence and his hoss pistol."

"Look here! Did Vincent pass himself off on Houston, too?"

Durant broke out in quick anxiety. "The scoundrel's capable of any sort of story—"

"I don't guess he took the time," Hittel rejoined. "He was arter Faith and that gold, and things were in a flurry around there. But yonder's Sam—the damned old wet-nurse! Yonder—back o' that tent. You can ask him your own self."

They had risen and walked on. Sentinels; questions; then the man himself. A lone figure seated on a saddle, feet insulated from the wet ground by a block of wood. Draped in a blanket, Indian fashion. From under his bedraggled wool hat Houston was turning the pages of a book that rested on his knees; the "Commentaries" of one Cæsar.

So came the word of the Goliad massacre.

No chance to ask about Vincent; no need. Evidently, old Hittel had kept mum about his private affairs; the matter of the gold remained unknown. Houston, like every other man in camp, was carried away by what Durant reported.

"Murdered in cold blood!" Houston's booming voice lifted without reserve. "Let it be known! A man named Kerr brought news of the surrender. I planned to attack Sesma, but half my men ran away. Sesma was fronting me, Urrea at my rear; I had no transport for my wounded in case of defeat." Houston spoke as though delivering an oration. Men were gathering, coming on the run as the news of Goliad spread. At their generally hostile looks, Durant suddenly realized that Houston was speaking at them, not at him.

"With Fannin and his men slaughtered," he went on, "if this army here falls in defeat, the fate of Texas is sealed! For that reason, I shall retreat until I'm able to meet the enemy in battle and conquer them."

Houston dabbed at his red nose with a bottle of ammonia. He gazed about, his defiant gaze seeking challenge. None came. A few men sniggered, the majority paid no heed; they were repeating the Goliad news, seeking more details. Houston went on.

"I've vainly petitioned the Texas government for cannon. The government's fled to Harrisburg, increasing the senseless panic among the settlers. The general of the Texan army hasn't even a blanket," and the voice rose louder, the eyes roved more angrily. "He had a very good one to shelter him from the storms, but some scoundrel stole it and he had to borrow another. Evilly minded persons say I'm marching for the Red River and the Louisiana frontier. False, sir; that is false! We've marched up the Brazos to this position where we can get a supply of corn and beat the enemy ten to one, if he tries to cross."

NO ENTHUSIASM could be whipped up. A few oaths and grunts made response. Houston sensed the futility of his words and turned more directly to Durant.

"Hittel, eh? I remember; he complained that his daughter is lost. Well, sir, I cannot find her. It's the young lady you are interested in, as I recall. I can help no one. I gave my last fifty dollars to two destitute women back at the Colorado; I'm reduced to one threadbare coat and a bed on the wet ground. Well, sir, you shall remain on my staff, subject to scouting service with Deef Smith. And now—details, details! Tell us what happened! Omit nothing! How did Fannin's men die?"

Durant cast aside his reserve and talked.

The Texan army? There were only five hundred men here, after all; Durant realized this with a sense of shock. True, the news from Goliad provoked a momentary hot, rapid wave of fury; then it passed, with a backwash of apathy. Of this army he found himself now a part, an aide to Houston nominally. But the realities were appalling.

To Durant, with nowhither to go, no faintest clue to follow, no trail to scent, this pitiful, hopeless, lost little army of Texas was a mere shadow, a mockery. The scenes among which he passed seemed as some evil dream.

The dreary skies closed down again to sodden heart and drown hope. The camp site became an island in the midst of swamps flooded by rain and the spreading Brazos. Five hundred men grumbling, cursing, living on corn from the fields, clearing the brush, foraging, growing webbed feet, huddled dripping around smoky fires and sleeping under drenched blankets.

Martial music of fitting accord. The fife and drum someone had fetched along. Orchestral notes of bullfrogs, owls and thunder-pumpers. The one song that all hands seemed to know and be able to sing, a song chanted often enough in bitter jibing voices, and yet destined, ere long, to a strange accolade of fame:

> *"Will you come to the bower I have shaded for you?*
> *Your bed shall be roses bespangled with dew.*
> *Will you, will you, will you, will you*
> *Come to the bower?"*

Old Hittel, with weeping eyes and nose and beard, impoverished of gal and gold, wandering like a lost soul from mess to mess with his lamentation of whining woes, his frightened unvoiced secret of the gold.

The company from Kentucky, the Newport Volunteers, with their captain and lieutenant-colonel in gallant blue roundabout trimmed with silver lace, somewhat the worse for weather. Their Texas flag of heavy white silk bordered with gold fringe; upon its field a torch-upholding Goddess of Liberty, the staff topped by a glove of the gallant captain's sweetheart. Growling, mutinous men everywhere cursing the rains, the swamps, above all the man who led them.

Houston unshaven for weeks, wearing thin and seamy old black frock coat, snuff-colored pantaloons tucked into cowhide boots, drooping wool hat minus its feather; his betasseled dress saber in rusty scabbard belted to his waist by a buckskin thong; sleeping only by snatches Cæsar's work and "Gulliver's Travels" his only solace; hartshorn bottle constantly at his nose to exercise the malaria.

MEASLES AND malaria, malaria and measles, everywhere. A sorry camp, a rabble outfit and leader, despair gnawing at every heart, and Texas lost, gone glimmering.

The plaintive choked bawls of cattle, when cattle were found, with quick-cut throats; a bloody meat spiraled on ramrods and held into smoky blaze; whiskered men champing and bolting the half-raw rations. Drills, with that voice of Houston ringing savagely; drills by company battalion and regiment, the men rebelliously sloshing about, ever with the sullen mutterings and outspoken threats. What realities—what awful realities were here!

Colonel Ben Smith, adjutant general, announcing: "I wouldn't blow my own horn boys; but I've always believed that if God Almighty intended me for anything it was for a military commander." Sullen laughter of hell bubbling up. And Santa Anna pushing for the Brazos at San Felipe with 1,400 men, infantry cavalry and artillery! Not to mention the other columns of his outflung forces; Lord knew where they were.

The realities began to grow farcical, provoking Durant to frantic, wondering questions. Before dawn each morning, Houston beat the reveille himself, three taps on the drum; at dark each night tattoo was sounded by the same hand, to put the army to bed. Durant realized how here one man was against an army.

The steam tug Yellowstone, from the Gulf, lay at Groce's plantation landing. Rumor said that, instead of loading cotton, she was to take the army across for another retreat. A few recruits from east Texas straggled in to join the force. Two iron six-pounders, a gift to Texas from the people of Cincinnati, had been landed on the Gulf coast and were coming on, if anyone could haul them.

The army began to take cheer. Fight—why not? With the cannon, and a fighting leader, anything might be possible. Sherman, captain of the Kentucky outfit, would make a good leader. There was talk of election, of the whole army volunteering to follow Sherman.

Then one morning, Durant stood over two graves, freshly dug and awaiting occupants, and read the scrawled notice pegged to a tree: "The first man beating up volunteers from the army will be court-martialed and shot. Sam Houston, Com'dr-in-Chief."

There was no election. But instead came a dispatch from the President of the Republic of Texas, who was on the run:

> Sir: The enemy are laughing you to scorn. You must fight them. You must retreat no farther. The country expects you to fight.

One man against an army; now, against a country. Houston published an order for all to read: "The moment for which we have waited… is fast approaching. The victims of the Alamo and the spirits of those who were murdered at Goliad call for cool, deliberate vengeance… The army will be in readiness for action at a moment's notice."

Action? It was elsewhere. The thunder of cannon rolled up the tawny Brazos—the Rio de los Brazos de Dios, it had been. The Mexicans were forcing a crossing at San Felipe! Houston, hoping for the Cincinnati cannon, loudly vowed it was impossible. Every boat had been seized, and the river ran too high for fording. The cannon voices died. By the next news, the enemy force had retired, Houston was right.

A FEW more recruits came in. With them, the Twin Sisters, the cannon from Cincinnati; but the sisters had lost their fodder somewhere. The smithy at Grace's began to ring with hammer and chisel cutting log chains, horsehoes, scrap iron into bits and filling cotton bags with the improvised shrapnel.

Still the rain, everlasting. Then two prisoners came in. Durant and Deef Smith, one scout brought two Mexican deserters. They talked willingly enough, on the way, of the column from which they had skulked.

"It is General Ramirez y Sesma with fourteen hundred men; and His Excellency, *El Presidente* himself. Other troops are coming behind. His Excellency is in haste to cross this River of the Arms of God, and to catch up with your general who runs away."

They found a new face in Houston's tent, when they turned over the captives—that of Colonel Tom Rusk, secretary of war, come to take a rifle. Durant left the conference at headquarters and joined old Hittel, crouching at a fire and wolfing some food. After a time Deef Smith joined them.

"Santy Anna's smart. Heading the middle column to cross Brazos, strike for the Trinity. Swing north. Cut us off, and settlers. The other columns will pocket us."

"Nonsense," snorted Durant. "Santa Anna hasn't crossed the Brazos yet!"

"Plenty holes," grunted Deef Smith. "Say! Rusk says ol' Man Hittel's gal is at Harrisburg."

Faith in safety? Then she must have shunted Vincent somewhere; he could be run down when occasion offered. Old Hittel reared to hind legs at this news.

"What say? How fur to Harrisburg?"

"Nigh sixty mile."

"We'll be goin', Durant! Are ye ready?" declared the old man excitedly. "She outsmarted that skunk; I reckon she has the money. If she ain't—by Gawd, what ye standin' there for? Gimme your hoss if ye ain't got the spunk. I'm goin' if I have to foot it, hear me?"

"No use," Durant said, impassive. "Orders are that no one leaves camp."

The old man cursed, wavered, then sank down, submerged in impotent fury.

"Them Mexicans will cross and git ahead of us!"

"We're crossin' first," said Deef Smith, jerking a thumb toward Houston's tent. "Right quick. Retreat."

"Once we're acrost," raved Hittel, "Sam Houston and his hull army ain't stopping me from finding my gal! She'll know where that money is—"

The gold, Durant thought sardonically, would be with Vincent, not with Faith.

Deef Smith was right; orders came sharp and fast. The army fell to frantic work, crossing the Brazos by means of the cranky Yellowstone. They crossed, waited here for orders, for news. Marking time again.

Faith at Harrisburg—ill—in need? And Vincent—damnation! Vincent at liberty, capable of anything!

From the plantation smithy came the clink-cling of hammer and chisel, chiming to the words of old Hittel's wrathful appeal. Durant was scowling, rebellious, angry. The camp was fretful with discord, Sam Houston was bulking larger with his huge, obstinate patience. Then, abruptly, Karnes came in with hurried word.

"Hey! Santy Anna's got a regiment acrost, thirty mile downriver—cavalry and artillery crossing. Hellbent for Harrisburg to ketch the government—"

The Mexicans across!

Durant's horse was already saddled and waiting some order. He broke into life, whipped around, came upon Deef Smith.

"Where ye off to?"

"Harrisburg. Tell old Hittel I'll get news of his daughter. And tell Houston I'm gone—"

Durant swung into the saddle and was gone, leaving the deaf scout to stare after him, slack-jawed.

CHAPTER XII

HITTEL'S END

THE ROAD, no more than a pair of ruts through soggy prairie, was a quagmire from the rains. The horse frequently sank almost to his hocks before tugging free. Everywhere were symptoms of panic, the whole countryside in flight; here, too, was the bulk of the general refugee mass. Settlers' outfits were overtaken, bogged down and frantic, or painfully toiling on. Questions were hurled at Durant from every side.

"Be you from the army?"

"Has the Mexicans crossed yet, stranger?"

"Is Houston a-coming? He said for us folks to keep ahead of him."

At a crossroads junction the trail forked, northeast and easterly. A farmer stood here beside the gateway in his rude fence, directing the stream of refugees. Durant, noticing that they all turned for the left, stayed his lathered mount.

"Which trail for Harrisburg?" he queried.

"Right-hand fork, stranger. It'll take you to Harrisburg straight as a compass. Left-hand road is for the Trinity and the States. Where's Houston?"

"Back at Groce's on the Brazos. Getting ready to march," replied Durant.

The settler shook his head. "God help him if he takes that left-hand road—he'll have no army! I left him when he retreated from the Colorado, to look after my family. Now we're all waiting to see which way he jumps. You're the second man in two days to ask for Harrisburg—most are on the dead run."

"Will I have any trouble in following the road?"

"Nope. Keep on across the prairie to the south. You'll skirt Buffalo Bayou and hit a trail below, from the Brazos to Harrisburg."

Durant spurred on alone.

This night he made solitary camp in a deserted cotton gin amid the wreckage of flight. At daybreak he saddled up and pursued the phantom of Harrisburg, Faith, Vincent. The going became better when he turned upon a trail pointing east—the one of which he had been told.

The prairie lands of this lower country were lovely with the warming sun of spring. They spread out like an Eden—but one all open to vandal foot and hand. The peace of a silence brooding upon the coming morrow had succeeded to anguished protests of fugitives young and old, their harried animals and lurching vehicles.

All this day, Durant spurred hard. Toward night, when dusk filled the air, he was aware of the salty breath of the Gulf floating in upon the air, tainted with the savor of marsh and bayou. Buffalo Bayou should lie off to his left. At a bridge over a swollen, swiftly running creek, he found a rude sign, to be read in the rapidly thickening twilight: "Harrisburg, 3 mi."

A long three miles. Until, with squatty Harrisburg still merged from sight in the misted gloom, Durant's horse suddenly shied from something at the roadside. His hand darted to pistol-butt; but a voice arrested hand and bit.

"Stranger, howdy! Be ye going to Harrisburg?"

Durant reined in. That testy, feeble voice was unmistakable. Dismounting, he looked down on old Hittel.

THE OLD man lay flat on his back. His watery eyes stared up in the dusk, blinking and vacant. Then they widened with the dawn of recognition.

"Goddlemighty!" he exclaimed weakly. "Ain't that Gordon Durant?"

"Sure is. What the devil are you doing here? What's wrong with you?"

Hittel struggled to sit up, failed in the effort, and propped himself with one gaunt elbow. Mud-caked to his knees, draggled of beard and hair, his seamy visage sweat-grimed, he was a derelict indeed.

"Confound ye! I took it you warn't coming," he complained. "You said no one was to leave camp. I lit out to find my gal. Aimed to git track o' that gold. Faith wrote me she'd be waiting in these parts."

"Wrote you?" exclaimed Durant. "You got a letter from her?"

"Yep. Rusk fetched a letter from Harrisburg. Said she'd expect me there. Nary mention of the gold. I swapped my oxen for a mule and started off. I didn't calculate to ask anybody's permission; it's my business. Some skunk of a refugee stole my mule and I had to come along on foot."

Old Hittel flopped back. "I'm fair petered out," he quavered. "Can't go a step farther. Ain't had a bite to eat sence last night. And them yeller-bellies coming."

"Mexicans?" Durant's voice was sharply edged. "What about 'em?"

"Ain't you heard? It's the tell they've crossed the Brazos and are aiming to ketch the gov'ment in Harrisburg. They fooled a ferryman by calling in English for his boat. Anyhow, they're acrost."

"They'll not be here before morning," Durant thought swiftly. "I've seen no sign of 'em. It's two days' march from the Brazos; and Harrisburg will be on the watch. We'd better go along and find Faith. You take my horse. I'll walk."

"No use; I can't sit a saddle, can't even stand," said Hittel querulously. "You won't leave me?"

"Not yet, anyhow." Durant hesitated, then yielded. Advance scouts from the Mexican column might be along any time. The old man would be killed without mercy. "We'll move off the road. When you've eaten a bite and had a snatch of rest, we'll go."

"Thank'ee, Gordon. Faith wouldn't take it kindly if she l'arned you'd left me lyin' here with Mexicans coming. A snack to eat and a restin' spell, and I'll be prime and fit."

Durant half dragged, half lifted the old man, whose knees had given out, a little way from the road. Then he brought over his horse; and in the gathering darkness shared his scanty rations with Hittel. Half an hour's rest, he reflected, would be enough.

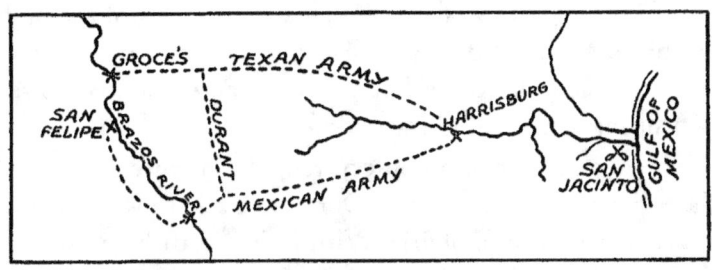

Old Hittel dozed off. Durant thought impatiently upon Faith, now so near, and listened to the man's breathing. The silence, save for the occasional stir of the horse near by, was profound. Insensibly, Durant yielded to it. A mere forty winks, perhaps, would do no harm—

Head drooping on breast, Durant slept.

Alarm in the night sprung him wide awake, all in an instant, with Indian swiftness. He was up and jumping for his horse, throttling the animal's nostrils. Jingle of spurs and bridles, clash of soldier arm, scuff and squeak of leather, clatter and pound of hooves; a dark column, riding at the trot, was passing, bulking large in the gloom.

Mexican dragoons, fifty at the least, riding for Harrisburg! Durant turned and felt for old man Hittel, called to him softly. No response. He was gone. The long roll of the thudding hooves died away in the murk.

"Hittel! Where are you? All's safe—" Reins in hand, Durant dared another summons. He strained all senses, felt no presence, heard no movement, no sound. The dragoons had made on, detached for night foray.

DURANT VAULTED into saddle. Now what of Harrisburg, and Faith? As he rode, he cursed the unexpected raid of the invader, cursed the old fool who had delayed him, only to mysteriously desert him. Wandered off, frightened off, perhaps taken to the road; but wherever the old man now was, his appearance and vanishment had complicated everything.

Ha! Durant suddenly drew rein. He might yet be in time to help Faith, to rally the townsfolk, to give warning of the raid! By the sounds, the dragoons had halted in the road ahead. Champ of bit, tinkle of steel, casual voices, all announced horsemen sitting at ease amid the darkness.

No shock of arms, no outcry, rent the night canopy over Harrisburg, down the bayou. Durant muzzled his horse and turned aside into the prairie. With Indian craft he moved silently, quickly, making the circuit of the squadron blocking his trail The dim sounds of massed men and horses fell behind and faded in the rear. Durant re-entered the trail and broke to a lope, for the soft and sandy soil deadened the hoof beats.

Sudden, frantic, he drove in spurs. Light ahead—aye, light! The thick horizon down the road had really blossomed, with swiftly mounting furnace glow. While Durant pelted on, the low roofs of little Harrisburg swept into sight, now illumined under swirling plumes of smoke mush-roomed in the upper air but shot with sparks and tongues of furious flame reflecting a ruddy light into the streets. Figures of men were on the run there. The dark surface of the bayou in front of the town borrowed the fiery glow and shimmered like a pool of blood.

Two, three houses all ablaze. No reports of rifles, no clangor of attack and defense, no sound of alarm. Then, almost too late, Durant again drew hasty rein in sharp dismay. The men busied in the streets were Mexicans—dismounted dragoons, searching, looting, bustling about. So Harrisburg was taken!

And Faith? That must be seen to. The dragoons were few in number. Any prisoners would be herded to one side in safety, under guard. One whole portion of the town was still dark. Yes, it was possible.

Pistols uncovered and loosened in their boots, Durant picked his way forward, his horse restive under the crackling sweep of flames. Still he heard no lamentations, no outcry of voices, no battle notes. Only the shouts of the pillaging dragoons reached him. He saw only these hustling figures, made infernal from the snapping flames of hell, and himself made cautious progress.

Now he was looking into the small square, flanked by a blazing roof. He had come as far into the town as possible—but no! He alertly tightened rein. The flame-lit square was boiling with an eddy of confused shapes. A knot of dragoons were fast to a prisoner. A graybeard, draggling hair redly stained; a prisoner struggling, resisting, buffeted with fists and musket butts, struck down, dragged on amid shouts and oaths and laughter.

Old man Hittel there. With a final hearty shove and kick he was sent reeling, to fall full length and desperately try to front about, rising like a defiant, stricken eagle. The ribald squad stood off and waited. An officer had been called.

FOR DURANT, suddenly everything went smash. Murders—the ashes of the Alamo, a stink in his nostrils—the cries ringing from the Goliad prairie—the wild faces of men murdered in cold blood—everything boiled up in him past bearing. His brain paused not to reckon. He sent his horse forward from the darkness. He struck in spurs as he plunged into the lighted square, and with shake of rein came charging.

Mexican eyes were quick. Cries of surprise and challenge, shouts of alarm, guns caught up and lances glittering. But Durant was not charging those dismounted men. His course was straight for old Hittel, blindly tottering on his feet.

Leaning, with swerve of horse and wrench of bit, but with

pace scarce slackened, Durant had the old man in grip. He caught the old thin figure under armpits, hoisted him clear and swung him up, dragging the clawing shape across the saddle. Then, with muskets bellowing after him and balls whining, he went tearing for the open. Barely in time, the utter madness in his brain had been checked. Barely in time he had headed for the lone, bleeding old figure, instead of sweeping into those murderers.

No pursuit for the moment. He readjusted the panting, cursing figure across his saddle. No sign of Faith or other prisoners. Harrisburg had been evacuated in time, thank Heaven!

Then voices, a pounding of hoof beats, sudden appearance of men around. Dragoons, some patrol bursting upon him unexpectedly. A shape loomed before him with alarm shout. They were everywhere—he was caught.

"Texas!" leaped out his Indian yell. "Texas!"

Pistol leaped out, countered saber blow, Madness swirled into him again. The pistol roared. Durant leaned forward, gripped, tore away the saber. The body of old Hittel supported him. The other pistol roared. Saber in hand, he was among them, and they, disconcerted, not dreaming a lone man here, broke into wild yells. The saber smashed down, smashed and cut again, again. Rearing horses, screaming men. Then an opening and darkness. The horse headed into it, with more sense than the man. A lance pricked his flank and drove him to gallop. Durant senses still unleashed, was carried off into the darkness.

His brain wakened. He rode on, and presently came to sanctuary amid the marshy growth of the bayou. Any pursuit now would be vain and fruitless. He eased the horse in among the trees, swung to earth and lifted down the shivering old man.

Hittel spoke faintly but coherently.

"No use, Gordon. By damn, I took ye for a Mex! No use. We can't go back."

"No need to go back," said Durant. "I've seen enough. Tell

me where you're hurt. I'll bandage you, and we'll backtrail with word—"

"Nope. I'm past mending. Head's slashed, but I got a lance in my belly. I fought 'em best I could—" He paused, gathered breath, went on. His story brooked no delay. "I found 'em in town. Left you asleep and went on foot. Three fellers there, printers, at the newspaper shop. Everybody else had lit out. Faith was aiming to leave with 'em. They had a boat—"

"Faith?" burst out Durant, incredulous. "You mean Faith's there?"

"Yep. She was asleep. She'd scarcely woke up when them dragoons came busting in. I tell ye, they got her! They got my gal—" The old man strove to sit up, shuddering as with a chill. Durant, supporting him, sensed the touch of warm blood everywhere, sensed the writhing agony of the man. "I had notion to—to ask Faith about—that gold—lay me down. I can't breathe—"

Durant lowered him. This seemed to give relief. He maundered on, his words crowding to escape ere his lips failed.

"Git out," he gasped. "Go tell Sam Houston I know he's hidin' up in the bresh, and soon's I git done with these land robbers down here, I'm comin' to smoke him out."

"Eh?" Durant thought the old brain was wandering, but not so. "What you mean?"

"He said that. Him—that officer. Said to tell Sam Houston."

"What officer?" demanded Durant.

"I dunno. They called him Excellency—no matter." The old fingers, icy cold, clutched Durant's arm with a burst of fierce energy. "Tell Sam Houston they got my gal and killed me. Fetch him down here if he aims to fight—you find Faith—she's yourn—"

Hittel's hand dropped. He sighed and relaxed, and was at peace.

DURANT SAT there, in a seething scald of emotions.

Excellency! Then Santa Anna in person had been with these dragoons. Regret, that he had not gone on and found Faith, instead of sleeping; there would have been time. Wrath at himself, for having slept; at Hittel, for not having waked him. Wrath rekindled, at Vincent. That accursed gold! It had brought only death and trouble. Faith, caught in the toils, he had missed her. Faith!

Durant settled down, after loosing the cinched girth of his horse, to a sleepless vigil beside the dead man, until daylight came to aid him. The glow over Harrisburg waned and died as the fires spent themselves and the embers dulled.

The sullen sky above prairie and swamp and bayou brightened at last with daybreak. Durant was in the act of seeking a spot to swim across, when he quickly caught the nostrils of his horse again, stood tensed, peering through the leafy covert. The road came close to the bayou, here, only a few yards away.

Troops, almost within lance-reach. Infantry, marching at will in solid column; the officers were mounted. A brass field-piece rolled behind its caisson and mule-span. Durant hauled down his horse's nose. Safe for the moment, at least.

The column passed, with hasty shuffle, muskets shouldered, pannikins clinking, all faces intent on the lazy smudge that announced Harrisburg ahead. Now the sky was suffused with the brassy sheen of sunrise. A garish light struck level upon prairie, road and column.

In the rear of the column came the prisoner squad—deserters, thieves, whatnot; these infantry regiments were composed largely of convicts. And from these, straggling under guard, one man looked forth toward the bayou, as though with quick calculation of chances if he made a break for it. His face was clearly defined in the hard highlight reflected from the sunrise sky. The man, arms bound and under close guard—

Durant stifled the cry half-wrenched from his lips, a cry of wild rage, savage glee, disappointment. Joy for the scoundrel now promised his just deserts. Disappointment that he himself was bilked of vengeance. Rage that he must stand here and see the man march past almost within reach, and vengeance unsatisfied.

For that man was Vincent Durant, his half-brother!

Faith and Vincent, now both in Harrisburg, with Santa Anna! And the gold as well? This was yet to be learned; no matter. He might lose it and Vincent, but he was not going to lose Faith. Threescore cavalry, a piece of artillery, six to seven hundred infantry—well, others might cope with these. Santa Anna was with them. News here for Sam Houston!

Buffalo Bayou flowed fifty yards wide or more, darkly deep, swollen to swiftness by the rains. Durant moved, led his horse, breasted out for the other bank. He must risk being seen by any stragglers.

Presently he staggered out, mounted dripping into the saddle, and headed away. No sparing the horse now! A terrible impatience flogged him on and on with bloody spur. On across the miles, and on, ever on....

FROM AFAR the sound reached him, thin and faintly pulsating. Gusts of rain had been falling most of this day. Now it had ceased, and the sound took form and tune. Voices swelled it.

"*Will you come to the bower?*" The army of Texas was on the march.

Here was the road-fork, where stood the solitary settler's farm; but the settler was gone now. When Durant came trotting in, the music had ceased and the column had halted in confusion. Which way? The few refugees had already pelted out along the road to the left, for the eastern frontier. Deef Smith and Red-head Karnes were consulting, midway between the forks.

Durant's voice rose in furious direction. A yell from the ranks made reply.

"Right-hand fork, boys! That's ourn!"

The music of fife and drum struck up anew. The men waited for no orders but swung around. The drenched files, with the

Goddess of Liberty wetly braving the leaden sky above, pitched off on the Harrisburg road.

General Houston was soaked and hunched under his big hat. Durant came up to him.

"I've been to Harrisburg, general. It's occupied by Santa Anna and a column. I saw a field-piece, six to seven hundred infantry, less than a hundred dragoons. The town was set afire. It had been abandoned, except by three or four persons."

Houston's blue eyes were thoughtful and serene and somber, as though no longer perplexed. The man appeared deep in one of his fits of meditation.

"To Harrisburg, eh? On private business?"

Durant assented. Houston smiled; a knowing man, this. In his ponderous but piercing way, a reader of the heart.

"You found the young lady?"

"The business is unfinished," said Durant, his lips compressing for an instant. "She was caught by the Mexican advance, I believe. Her father was killed. I'm heading back."

"You'll have company this time. The army's chosen its road. By God, if they want a fight, they'll get one!" He lifted his voice in one of his oratorical pronouncements, so that the ringing words swept down the files. "We know the enemy has crossed the Brazos and marched for Harrisburg; but they're treading the soil on which they're to be conquered. I'll fight them in a place of my own choosing. I intend to conquer and put to flight the entire Mexican army, and it shan't cost me a dozen of my men."

A voice from the marching files broke in, laughingly.

"That's right, gin'ral! No easy-goin' scrimmage for us."

Houston turned to Durant. "You say Santa Anna himself is there?"

"I believe so. Before old Hittel died, he spoke of some insulting message—"

"I've received it already, delivered by the damned black who helped 'em across the river," broke in Houston. "All right. Now we'll flush the whole covey!"

Cursing the two cannon, which had bogged down, Houston went at a gallop to help the men put their shoulders to the wheels. Karnes, the captain of scouts, rode on with Durant, and spoke his mind.

"The old man spouts like he was addressing all Texas, including the Mex army! That's Injun council-fire talk. What this army wants is fight, not speechifying. Near had a rumpus and another commander, back a piece; no one knew where we were heading for. Wily Martin's company voted to quit and go look after their families. To my notion, old Sam has been straddling the fence to save his bacon if anything goes wrong."

"Maybe he's been waiting to get Santa Anna out on a limb," Durant barked. The Houston of the Horseshoe Bend battle, and of Cæsar's "Commentaries," was neither fool nor coward. Karnes gave him a sharp, quick look.

"Maybe so. Well, if Santa Anna's out on the limb, we'll have to beat him to the crotch. Maybe Sam knows where he's going and why. We sure don't."

The rain continued through the day; but Durant sensed a change now in the spirit of the army. A few recruits had come in from scattered points.

Eight hundred in all, two field pieces, fourteen wagons, marching in rain and prairie mud, but cheerful about it. Wagons and gun carriages sunk to the axles; Houston, stripped of his black coat, took turn at the wheels, tugging like an ox at the ropes, shouldering baggage when loads had to be lightened. He was a man of volcanic energy, now slumbrous, now erupting in torrential bursts.

The men were light-hearted again, despite rain, despite retreat, despite everything. Fighting at last—no more running! And pretty near on even terms, too, according to Durant's news.

CHAPTER XIII

"THE RIGHT MINUTE"

FORTY-FIVE MILES in two and a half days of plugging, hauling, sweating work, and of tentless bivouacs.

Buffalo Bayou lay glassy under the thinly veiled high sun. The breeze from the Gulf, twenty miles eastward, scarce stirred the live oaks that bordered the bayou and dotted the prairie sea with islets. The lingering smoke of burned Harrisburg hung upon the horizon, ominously. This camp of the Texan army was the haven of exhausted men, outstretched like the dead.

The general had taken another spurt, but whether he was trying to catch Santa Anna or to beat him across the Trinity in further retreat, only Houston knew. The men were furious, resentful, sullen, ripe for mutiny. Unless he fetched up for a fight at once, they would put Rusk or Sherman into command.

Durant's eyes flitted back and forth. He was glad to be out of that sullen camp, glad to be off on scout with these men: Deef Smith, Karnes, Captain Dick Handy.

Harrisburg, opposite, smoked in ruin. No moving figure there, nor in all the landscape. The enemy had vanished; and, with them, Faith and Vincent. This was not the end of trail for him.

"What d'ye say, Deef?" blurted Handy. "They've skipped."

"East'ard to lower Trinity. Rouse the Injuns."

"Damned lot of rascals in them bay parts, too," Karnes said. "The gin'ral done sent a commission to treat with the Injuns. They won't rouse."

Deef Smith shook his head. "Injun jump to strongest side. Look for plunder."

"That Galveston country's powerful mean," grumbled Handy. "All cricks and bayous and swamp. Well, let's git back to the gin'ral."

Back to camp, empty of news. Houston appeared to be the only person awake in the whole camp. He was seated, poring over a tattered map. He did not look up as the four men grouped around; merely halted his tracing finger and spoke.

"No news?"

"Nope," Deef Smith replied. "Town burned, everybody gone. Any orders?"

"Curse this map! It's a travesty on the face of Texas," Houston growled.

He laid a broad thumb on the area east and southeast of Harrisburg. The thumb covered the area of Buffalo Bayou to its union with the San Jacinto, covered the angle formed by the bayou and the river that emptied into Galveston Bay.

"There's the enemy. They've chased the government to the bay and are probably expecting other columns to join them. They'll undoubtedly cross the San Jacinto at Lynch's ferry to continue eastward."

"Just my notion, gin'ral," approved Deef Smith.

"We must get ahead of them," Houston continued, frowning at the map. "But our men need rest; and we must know exactly where the enemy are. Mr. Smith, you cross over this evening, with any companions you may need, and get that information."

"Right after siesta," and Deef Smith nodded. "Suits me. Mebbe pick me up a fresh razor strop."

"Eh?" Houston glanced up, and caught the implication. "You'll bring any prisoners to me, sir——with their hides intact! That's all."

HE RESUMED his intent study. Durant and the other three flung themselves down in shade and slept; the siesta hour,

in this country, was a necessity. The hazed-over sun was westering when Durant sat up to the dry accents of Deef Smith.

"Come on. Got to raft it over and swim the hosses. If I get
me a razor strop, I'll need dry powder. No objection to swimming back."

Talking was ended, argument done, in few words. Silent,
grunting an occasional oath, the four went to work at the edge
of the swollen bayou. Driftwood and dead timber were lashed
together. Durant, Karnes and Smith alone were going, Handy
remaining here.

They tested the makeshift raft and then pushed out, with a
pole and rudely fashioned paddles serving their way, and Handy
shooting caustic comment after them. The raft sank ankle deep,
then knee deep; the swimming horses came after, guided by
taut bridle reins. Somehow they reached the other bank, left
the raft in a cove of the Harrisburg shore, and mounted.

Again the trail, again hand to knife, powder-horn ready, eyes
alert. Durant took heart and hope. If he was serving Houston
and liberty, he was serving himself first of all.

In the twilight they picked up the trail east from Harrisburg.
Foot, hoof and wheel; infantry, cavalry, pack mules, field pieces,
heading away. And with them, thought Durant, a fair-haired
girl and a scoundrel.

"One march to the San Jacinto and Lynch's ferry," said
Karnes. "The gin'ral was right."

"Trail's twenty-four hour old," Deef Smith croaked. "Plaguey
long head start."

"Mebbe they've gone visiting south to New Washington,"
said Karnes. "Rich country, plenty plunder."

"Might be," agreed Deef. "We could ketch up at the ferry,
have a scrimmage. What say, Durant? Your gal's with 'em. Sneak
her out. Your say-so."

A friendly offer here, but Durant held himself in leash.
Serving himself first? Thought of the lonely man tracing lines
on the map halted him.

"Nope. Thanks all the same," he said. "Houston needs information. Neither army knows where the other is. If we get Santa Anna, we win everything. Can't be selfish, Deef. We'd lose time following this trail in the dark; but there'll be deserters, sure, looters and plunderers. Men stealing off to forage. If we lie low, we'll get what Sam Houston wants."

"There's sense in that," Karnes approved. "The greasers have no idea the army's reached the bayou. They'll be careless. What say, Deef?"

"Tie the hosses in timber," said Deef Smith. "Henry, you and Durant take 'em. I'll be up the road a piece."

He suited action to words, and presently slipped away in the darkness. Durant made fast the horses, then rejoined Karnes near the trail, where stumpage and long grass afforded cover. They would be certain, with patience, to pick up deserters or couriers.

SUDDENLY KARNES vented a warning hiss.

Already Durant had turned ear to the faint jingle, the soft sound growing into the pit-a-pat of horses at the trot. On the very instant came a sharp hail in Spanish, then oath supplementing oath in English, followed by a chatter of alarm and fear.

"All right. Deef's got 'em!" exclaimed Karnes, and the two men broke into a run.

Deef Smith had them, right enough, in full blaze of moonlight. Two riders at the muzzle of his long rifle. The one, a Mexican officer; the other, an *hombre* in common private's garb. Both of them now dismounted, cautiously.

"Keep 'em covered." Deef Smith handed his rifle to Karnes. "I'll take a look in them saddle bags."

The two stood motionless. Durant, pistol ready, covered the private, who was staring hard at him. A stammer of incredulity broke from the man.

"You, *señor?* But then, you have escaped?"

Recognition jogged Durant. Why, Juan, of course—Juan, partner of the jaunty dead Jacopo! He who had escorted Doña Amadora to Refugio; he whom Durant had met in the night and left bound on the prairie! And this fellow, of El Tuerto's gang, was now in uniform, a soldier. Suddenly Durant felt Vincent very close to him.

"So! You recognize me?"

"But yes, *señor!* Only this morning I saw you in the prisoner squad—"

A sudden choked, angry bawl from Deef Smith thrashed all else aside.

"Karnes! Durant—lookee here—" The words subsided into oaths, as Smith extended the saddle bags he had removed.

They were of deer hide. On the flaps was written a name in black letters, distinct and clear in the moonlight: "Col. Wm. Barret Travis." Spoil from the Alamo—the saddle bags of Travis himself.

"By God!" came a thick growl from Karnes.

The pair of bags fell from Deef Smith's hand. He whipped out his knife. His cold stare traveled from captive officer to man, and back again.

"Here's where I cut me a couple razor strops," he barked, but Karnes intervened.

"Wait, Deef! Wait! We got to take 'em across. After the gin'ral's done talking with 'em, it'll be our turn. See what's in those bags."

Deef Smith hesitated. The officer spoke up calmly, with never a quiver.

"*Señores,* I am a courier in uniform, with despatches. Are you murderers?"

The fellow Juan, however, took the matter otherwise and dropped to his knees.

"No Alamo! I was not there. I will tell all, all! No Alamo!"

"I've seen you before." Karnes surveyed him critically. "At

Bejar. You're one o' them Mexicans who 'listed for Texas a year and a half back, then skipped out."

"I'm a guide, *señor!*" babbled the man in terror. "I was sent this morning to meet a courier from the west and lead him to His Excellency."

"Santa Anna? Where is he?"

"At a place called Nuevo Washington. He has seven hundred infantry, fifty cavalry, and one cannon. Twenty miles. We did not know Los Tejanos were near—"

"Where's he heading for?"

"How should I know, *señor?* But he is at the bay, *señor*; he must cross the San Jacinto if he is to go on east."

KARNES TURNED to the officer, the scowling Deef Smith hanging fire on all these questions, while looking into the saddle bags.

"And you? Where from?"

"From General Don Vicente Filisola."

"Where's he at?"

"You will excuse me from answering," said the officer haughtily.

"Don't matter, Henry," broke in Deef Smith. "He'll talk later. We got Travis' bags, stuffed with letters. Good ketch."

Durant swung around to the man Juan, caught his collar, and lifted him erect.

"Look at me! You think you know me?"

The frightened man stared, then jerked backward.

"*Diablo!* You are he—you are not the same—you're another—not Don Vicente—"

"Right. What do you know about an American girl who was taken prisoner at Harrisburg? Is she with the column now?"

"A girl with hair of maize? But yes, *señor*. She is for His Excellency, it is said. She is well treated and unhurt."

Durant caught his breath. For Santa Anna, eh? He knew the

repute of that lecherous little dark man; well, nothing could be done about it now. It was for Santa Anna to answer later.

"Let's go." Deef Smith threw the saddle bags over his shoulder. "Fetch 'em along. That raft won't carry but three. They can row me acrost. You can swim."

An hour later the Texan camp seethed, while Captain Moses Bryan, squatted beside a hastily primed fire, translated aloud the dispatches for the brooding, silent Houston and for all who crowded around. Those letters made everything simple.

Santa Anna had made wild-goose chase to Harrisburg, failed to bag the government of Texas by scant minutes, had gone on to the bay. Filisola was back at the Brazos, forty-five miles away, and was sending reinforcements. Urrea's column was at Matagorda, many a mile distant. Gaona's column had not yet crossed the Brazos. Houston and the Texan army were in wild flight and lost. So ran the word.

"By God!" muttered somebody. "Santy Anny's out on the limb, and the first comer can pot him! It's fish or cut bait now, all right!"

True. Here were other despatches from Mexico City, congratulating Santa Anna, the conqueror of Texas, the victor of the Alamo. Those titles ran through the crowd of listening men, but Houston made no sign.

DEEF SMITH, leaning on his rifle, malevolently eyed the prisoners. The officer had lost his mien of cool defiance. Men were muttering, cursing, grumbling. Houston was talking aside, with Rusk, in an undertone.

Durant, still wet with his swim, quivered with impatience. Seven hundred men ready to swim the bayou and leap at Santa Anna—and nothing happened, no orders given! Santa Anna out on a limb; the crotch at Lynchburg—nobody gunning for him? It was incredible. Had Houston gone mad?

So it seemed. Orders at last—to cross the bayou in the morning. In the morning! Why, it would take half the day for the army to get across—

Durant wandered away and sat down by himself, dropped his head in his hands, gave way to utter despair. He had lost faith in everything, in everyone. Houston had failed him, had failed the army, had failed Texas. Even now, these men should be streaming out to swim, run, march—reach the Mexican camp at all costs! Instead, they were to await the dawn, eating out their hearts, raging furiously and vainly.

And to Durant, it was Faith who was being lost. His iron restraint broke down. His pulses hammered. He started to his feet; how long he had been sitting, he knew not. Stiff, angry, in a mad tumult of emotion and despairing resolve, he stumbled toward the horses.

And abruptly, in the moonlight he came upon a huge figure standing alone, silent. The two of them were suddenly close, startled by each other. Houston, for a long moment, looked into the tortured, haggard features of Durant; but his own shaggy, grim countenance was strangely at rest and peace.

In the silence, an odd comprehension passed between them. Then Houston put out his arm and gripped Durant's shoulder.

"I know," came his deep, gruff voice. All oratorical affectation gone now. Here was the man alone. "I know. Looks like each one of us picks his own troubles, eh? Son, I got to think o' Texas. I got to pick the right minute—not the day nor the hour, but the minute. It ain't just win or lose, son. It's all o' Texas that gets won or lost, and forever. No second chance if we get beat. Hell! If it was my choice I'd be laying with Travis and Bowie or with Fannin; but we got to think of Texas. Just one card to play, and by God I'm going to play it at the right minute! And not until. Not—until."

The shaggy head lifted to the moonlight. The stooped, weary frame straightened. The patience, the loneliness, the astonishing inner strength of the man, all shone in his deep tired eyes, and then were lost in calm, assured confidence. A pat on the shoulder, and the big hand was lifted. The huge figure moved away and was gone.

Durant remained motionless for a long time, this strange memory deepening and hardening within him. Then he moved toward the nearest bivouac fire and stretched out for sleep. His impulses were gone.

CHAPTER XIV

"FIGHT AND BE DAMNED!"

MORNING ASSEMBLY, and Durant stared and listened in stark wonder. Was that memory of the lonely man in the moonlight all a delusion? For here was a different Houston, blustering, oratorical again—perhaps this was entirely a pose, after all! A pose, by one who knew the simple, forthright men around him.

"We will meet the enemy… trust God and fear not… remember the Alamo, the Alamo, the Alamo!"

The bayou had to be crossed, but no preparations had been made as ordered. A leaky scow, a plank raft. Houston himself hacking oars from fence rail; the stream running bank full and rapid from the rains. More slogging work, with the thought in every mind of Santa Anna out on the limb—and to be caught at the crotch or lost forever.

The water-logged scow got one baggage wagon across, the "Twin Sisters" and their caissons were rafted, the sixty horses were rushed to swimming depth and tolled on to the other shore. Little enough to brag about, but a day-long job. Twilight found the army across, a mob of hungry, cursing, fighting men— and no rations.

More delays now, Houston's voice booming again. How slow the dusk! At last the orders sounded, scouts were put out, the column was in forward march. Out of the timber and into the prairie again, upon the road to Santa Anna.

The night was starless, overcast, dark. No one knew what

Houston intended, whither he was going—bound to catch the
bear at the crotch, though! The thought upheld all hearts. Floor-
ing of bridge rattling underfoot, black water rushing beneath.

"Must be Vince's bayou," bleated Deef Smith. "Eight mile
to Lynchburg Crossing. Thar's the main crotch for our b'ar!"

The dawn crept up into a gray sky. The sky gradually softened
with rosy tints, borrowed from the sunrise lying like a ribbon
in the veil of the marsh mists. Then, sudden movement, voices,
a storm of orders. Horsemen were cantering smartly along the
road to the ferry, dragoons, lancers. Mexicans!

A dash across the angle, Durant spurring hard with Karnes
and the other scouts. Smith caught one of the laggards; the rest
spurred in flight and were gone. The scouts surrounded the
hapless Mexican.

"For the love of God, *señores*, do not kill me! We were on
patrol—the army is breaking camp and heading for the ferry.
If you ride farther you'll see the cavalry on the advance—"

"More'n you'll ever see," quoth Deef Smith, his knife out.

DURANT WAS pelting on the back trail again with the
news. The army had floundered all night. Now, in a patch of
woods the men were butchering cattle commandeered from
some ranch strays. Breakfast fires were crackling.

"Santy Anny's coming!" passed the word. "Heading up for
Lynch's ferry! How fur is that from here? Three mile? Drap
your meat, boys! Fall in, fall in!"

Forward! Santa Anna was coming back over his limb. Beat
him to the crotch!

The three miles fell behind. Scrawny Lynchburg and the
ferry lay across the river. Here Buffalo Bayou swung into the
San Jacinto. Here was a long swell of the lush prairie, bayou
and marsh and river all around save the direction of Vince's
bridge, eight miles westward!

Here was the amphitheater, with no enemy disputing it.
Cows in the grass—get a square feed this time, anyhow! The
race was won.

Durant saw little of it. He was off with Smith and Karnes, coursing the prairie crests along the San Jacinto marshes. The flashing wings of raucous wild fowl wheeled up, lance-points pricked through the tall grasses; the enemy's advance was feeling the road. Straight up for the ferry, blocked now by the Texan array.

Back now, pelting back for the last time with news. The Mexicans not a mile behind, Scouting done; the hour for close grips had struck.

The army was amid the oaks. Mess fires were smoking, the men licking hairy lips. A flatboat of Mexican flour had been captured. They squatted about fires, intent upon sizzling beef and browning doughballs, tearing ravenously at the food, gorging themselves.

Fall in, fall in! Durant loaded rifle, waited, saw the battle line formed up by Houston, lips dry and hands twitching.

But time passed. The morning advanced more rapidly than the enemy. The thin lilt of Mexican bugle calls filtered from the distance. The day waxed, and the day passed, impatience wrangled again with impatience. The afternoon waned.

Suddenly the Mexicans were coming forward, their cannon was opening fire. The "Twin Sisters" from Cincinnati smashed it with a round of horseshoe slugs. The Texas rifles drove the Mexican skirmishers to grass. Sherman led the mounted rifles out to capture the enemy cannon, but found none, and fell back under a hail of musketry. The twilight saw the "Twin Sisters" cooling, the Mexican line drawn back to the crest of a rise, across the open swale.

Incredulous, choking down his anger and dismay, Durant watched the Mexican supper fires winking along the dark reaches of the crest.

HE JOINED the men stoking themselves with baked dough and bloody beef, managed to make a meal, looked in vain for Deef Smith. The blanketed figure of Houston lay soles to fire-embers, head pillowed on cannon-rope, sound asleep.

Asleep now, this man who had so long gone sleepless! Now, of all times!

Later, a guard beyond the lines uttered challenge. Deef Smith came limping in from the darkness, paused beside Houston's snoring figure, and then passed on. Durant joined him with some beef, which the scout wolfed hastily.

"You'll find your gal in Santy Anna's tent. He's got a whopping big un."

"How do you know?" Durant exclaimed.

"Not so loud." Smith spoke in undertone. "Been on a prowl. Listened to picket talk. Cos is due from the Brazos tomorrow with five hundred men. Filisola comin' on with a couple thousand more. We're like to git pinched."

Durant whistled softly. "Houston gave orders not to waken him on any account, but—"

"Leave be," struck in Deef Smith. "The men were tuckered. Empty bellies. Vince's bridge'd ought to be cut down; that'd close the in trail from the Brazos. Tell Houston fust thing in the morning."

At daybreak assembly, Houston was still asleep. He slept through breakfast, and all hope of a dawn attack went glimmering, while the men stood to arms and cursed.

Houston slept until the sun struck down into his face—the first clear sunup in weeks. He was up, and the men stiffened eagerly. Attack? No! The damned old fool blinked at the sky, stared around, and talked like an orator: "The sun of Austerlitz has risen again!"

"Son of Austerlitz? Who in hell's that? Talks like the Scriptures," went the disgusted mutter.

Durant sat and listened and watched. If that bridge were cut, no reinforcements could reach Santa Anna. He saw Houston conferring with Deef Smith, obtaining this news of such importance; orders? Not a bit of it. Deef Smith chuckled, then went off and sat down with his rifle over his knees.

The sun mounted. Houston rambled about. The camp was

in a growl of impatience, officers and men conferring, cursing, eyeing Houston aslant. Durant fidgeted, rasped raw by the inaction. That lone man in the moonlight? Oh, hell; anyone with sense would smash these Mexicans now, before General Cos could arrive! The moonlight had made him fancy things.

A sudden triumphant roll of drums and peal of bugles; vivas, cheers mingled with the rub-a-dub and mellowed notes. The Mexican breastworks were alive with figures. A measured file of shapes came into sight, circling the end of the rise. Pack mules, by glory!

"There's them reinforcements, gin'ral," yelped Deef Smith for all to hear.

"A damned hoax," blared Houston. "Go and scout for yourself. Santa Anna's marching his men around and around, to hoodwink us."

Smith took horse and galloped away, to return presently and announce that the general was right. But men knew better. Already, rumors had spread and spread. They could see for themselves; Deef Smith had lied.

DURANT KNEW he had lied. A hell of a general, this was, to keep his eager men inactive while Mexican reinforcements poured in! Cos and his column should have been cut off. Santa Anna should have been attacked at dawn.

Under a moss-draped oak, Houston was holding a private confab with Deef Smith, who caught Durant's eye and beckoned repeatedly, Durant strolled across, unhurried, rebelliously. Deef Smith spoke softly, as he peered at Durant.

"Cos and four hundred men, all right; they're in the trap. Goin' to cut down that bridge. Need a good hand. What say?"

A swift, wild thrill coursed through Durant's veins. Trap! Going to cut the bridge now? Houston read his face and spoke, with a twinkle of the eye.

"Speed like eagles or you'll be back too late for the day," he said.

Eight miles to the bridge, barring interruption? The work

there, and back here again? No; no such throw of the dice for him. He had blundered too often before. Durant shook his head.

"Thanks," he said curtly. "I'm taking no chances on being too late."

Houston met his eye, chuckled, and nodded.

"Right; I forgot. Mr. Durant is excused, Smith; pick someone else."

Durant did not easily forget that keen, almost majestic glance; a man, here, of depths rarely fathomed, of friendship and understanding hard to comprehend.

Deef Smith and another, with axes, went away at the gallop, riding for Vince's Bayou and the lower prairie to the westward. Durant sat quivering, loading his pistols, suddenly upon a strain and tension that was unbearable.

Trap? Yes, of course. Cos in the trap too, with his men; all unwitting. Eleven hundred Mexicans, fully equipped, their backs to the San Jacinto marshes. Seven hundred and fifty Texans here, ill equipped, their backs to Buffalo Bayou. Not the day nor the hour, but the minute—what the devil had Houston meant by that?

Durant thrilled, and thrilled again. The bridge cut would mean two things—no more Mexican reinforcements, and no escape for any who were defeated. Durant's eyes flitted out past the grumbling, cursing knots of men, out to the crest yonder where Faith and Vincent awaited him. Vincent, to be found first if might be—

Not another soul here knew what was in the mind of Houston. A council of war was held; Houston listened gravely and said nothing. It was decided to oppose any attack on the Mexican line. The Texans were far out-numbered. They must charge across the open. The officers shirked such responsibility.

Houston held his peace. In the Mexican camp arms were stacked, picket lines sought their ease, officers and men dozed by their usual habit. Santa Anna composed himself for the siesta, upon his four-poster bed. The new troops had marched hard to get here; they dropped where they stood. The sacred hour of the siesta had come.

Sam Houston cocked an eye at the prairie rise. Deef Smith should be returning now. Mounting his white horse, Houston leaned forward, giving quizzical eye and ear to the squads of men who growled openly at him.

"Officers will parade their commands," he said suddenly, and clapped his hands as he rode forward. "Now fight and be damned!"

Durant jumped for his horse. The moment had come.

CHAPTER XV

THE TRAIL STRAIGHTENS

THE LONG loose line in double rank breasted the billowy green sea of waist-high grass, broke to pass the islets of oaks. Rifles were carried at the trail. Cannon horses tugged at the "Twin Sisters." Houston on his white horse led the center, and the white-and-gold flag of Kentucky Volunteers, with its lady's glove, fluttered in the breeze. Fife and drum struck up somewhere, and voices joined in.

"Will you come to the bower I have shaded for you?
Your bed shall be roses bespangled with dew."

The oaks were passed. No more cover now. Ages seemed to pass, as Gordon Durant pressed on to catch up with the forward files, a grim man enlisted in a war of his own. Almost incredulous, he realized that the ground was sloping upward now, that no sound of shot burst out ahead, no bullets whined.

The stacked muskets of the Mexican infantry, the silent barricade, formed a frieze against the skyline. Beyond that frieze—what?

Sudden excitement outburst. A bugle rang alarm. A sentinel fired wildly. White frightened faces appeared, figures half dressed, staring out at the approaching line. At the double now, men running madly, the rear files closing up. Lamar and his sixty cavalry were sweeping far out in a swing to turn the Mexican left and cut them off from any retreat.

Muskets began to spatter and spurt. The "Twin Sisters" had

halted now, swung about; suddenly they shook the air with a burst of powder and iron. The breastworks ahead began to shoot forth powder-smoke, bullets sang and whistled. A grimy horseman, ax in hand, crossed Durant's vision. It was Deef Smith.

"Vince's bridge is down!" he yapped out.

"Remember the Alamo!" blared Houston in the lead. The two little cannon had thundered again. The breastworks were smoking ahead; the white horse went down. The Texan rifles began to crack, and the mad yell arose that was to sweep through all Mexico for many a year with a shiver in its wake:

"Remember the Alamo! Remember Goliad!"

Houston found a mustang, mounted, gained the fore again with Durant close behind him. Over and into the thick of it with a spurring plunge and a roar; guns reversed, knives out, voices cracking. The wave struck and burst, and flowed on.

Durant drew rein briefly behind the barricade, upon a wild and bloody scene. Of combat there was little. Mexican soldiers upon their knees, shrieking out vainly. "Me no Alamo! Me no Goliad!" Fugitives ahorse and afoot flying in every direction. Houston in a frenzy, bareheaded, his right boot welling blood; Deef Smith, unhorsed, wielding pistol and bloody knife like any Apache.

Yonder, to the left, Durant had glimpse of a huge blue and white striped tent, with fringe and portico, set apart beneath a moss-hung oak. He wheeled his horse, then drew rein again. A mysterious warning finger plucked at him, pointed aside.

He looked off to the right. Mexicans ahorse and afoot were in flight here, as everywhere, but across the prairie lowland lay marshes and no escape. Then, close by, Durant realized the figure heading for the rout—a figure that signaled like a flag. Bareheaded, plying heels to stirrupless horse, riding like a Centaur; with a quick, eager pulse, Durant wheeled to the chase.

FAITH COULD wait; she would be cared for, would care for herself. First must come Vincent, and Durant struck in spurs. Not for him the slaughter that was taking place on every side! The rabid Texan yells, the shrieks and screams of Mexicans, the occasional burst of pistol or musket, drew him not.

Vincent was heading straight into the mad rabble of fugitives and pursuers, heading for the wide crescent of boggy savanna. A strapping volunteer, bounding on long legs, had reloaded his rifle without slackening pace—a border trick. He halted, braced, leveled the piece. Durant cried out sharply. He saw Vincent's horse stagger and lurch forward, and go kicking.

Then Vincent was up again, up and bending forward under a burden of saddlebags as he ran. A stream of fugitives crossed the trail, cut off Durant; he put his horse at them, cursing. A lance jabbed frantically at him, a knife pricked at his horse. He spurred on with hot oaths, breasted the tide of men, drew clear. Vincent was heading now straight into the swamp. Durant lifted voice in a long, wild yell.

Vincent heard it, turned about, staggered on and suddenly came to rest in a little patch of brush—flung down his burden, stood there panting, waiting. Durant spurred up, pistol in hand and cocked, then drew savage rein and flung off, watchful, before the cold, sneering gaze that greeted him. He stood wordless, exultant, his eyes like flame.

"I had ticketed you for hell, brother," came the mocking voice. Vincent was cool, defenseless, unarmed. The weeks had told on him. He was ragged, wolfish, stubble-bearded. "Well? Surely you don't balk at killing an unarmed man?"

"You're always armed with deviltry, damn you," said Durant harshly. No hurry about it; no mercy in his heart, either.

"And you alive and well? Come, come!" Vincent rejoined, between hot breaths. "I thought you dead and gone—"

His words died out. Even these men were impressed by the frightful scene around. Even the unshrinking heart of the one, the pitiless anger of the other, was momentarily quelled.

For the swamp, to right and left, was an inferno of bogged and sinking, shrieking humanity, of fugitives who recoiled from mud and water only to meet clubbed rifle and slashing bowie knife. Some clambered on over the bodies of those who were stuck fast, trod them down, fled on to be bogged in their turn. Knife and bayonet slashed in blood-mad lust of slaughter. Men and horses formed a bridge for others—a bridge to death beyond. Here and there was a little knot, where desperate men fought back before they were slashed down.

And amid these bushes, two men stood regarding one another, isolated in their sanctuary of private hatred.

"What about Faith?" Vincent spoke out suddenly, sharply. "You'd spare my life to know where she is, eh? No?"

Durant said nothing. He was unhurried now, sure of his prey, playing with the man before him, wringing him of evil, testing out the hatred and malice so soon to be a thing of the past. At his silence, Vincent laughed a little.

"Smart enough to nose me out, eh? How the devil you got out of those knots I tied—well, no matter now. Yes, the pretty Faith didn't stay long with me; she found out the mistake, damn her! Slipped away from me, but left me with the gold—until a Mexican patrol picked me up. The gold went into His Excellency's saddle bags—and I had my eye on them, you may be sure! Thanks to your Texan attack, I got them and a horse. And thanks to you—well, brother? Does the gold tempt you, eh?"

WELL PLAYED, thought Durant. The gold? He glanced down at the saddle bags, but his dark eyes did not soften. They struck back again at Vincent, uncompromising, grim, harsh, and Vincent shrank a little from the blow.

"You tempt me, not the gold," he said slowly, coldly. A light of terror sprang in the face fronting him, and was gone. The eager pistol stirred in Durant's hand.

"What? Ten thousand dollars?" quoth Vincent in bitter mockery. "It's your due, brother; what I took from our father when—"

"And ruined him," spat out Durant. "Killed him. Vincent, you've no decent shred of anything in the past; no single point of manhood."

"Why prate about it?" sneered the other. "But before you kill me and regret it, look at this—"

He stooped over, fumbling at the heavy, weighted saddle bags, plucking at the straps of tooled leather. Durant glanced at them.

Then, like a flash, Vincent struck. A knife darted from covert and struck out at the lithe body uncoiled. It was the strike of a snake, swifter than eye could follow. The numbing shock drove Durant backward, sent him off balance. His pistol exploded in the air. He plunged into the brush, headlong, rolled over, came to one knee.

He saw Vincent in saddle, bags flung across, the horse wheeling—his own horse! And then Vincent was gone.

Durant came to his feet. A hoarse, inarticulate cry burst from him. He gripped at the knife, still fast, and tore at it; not his own old knife, however. That was gone forever, no doubt. A thin, deadly Mexican knife, aimed for the space between neck and collarbone that means death; but haste had missed his coup de grâce.

With an oath, Durant tore the blade from its hot sheath. Knife in hand, he hurled himself forward, running, following the man and the horse. He could see the loose bags flopping; Vincent was at the gallop, yet so short had been the time that the space between them was not far.

Vengeance for the Alamo and for Goliad had been sated. It had left the lush grasses matted; the stream draining the bog was choked with bodies. In places, this little stream was entirely dammed by corpses that bridged it clear across. Once over this stream, a man might flounder on to hope of firmer footing beyond. Vincent evidently had this purpose.

The horse shied from the crimsoned, stinking marge. Shied violently, suddenly, with a wild snort of fear and dread. Vincent lost his grip, caught at the heavy burdened saddle bags, and was pitched from the saddle with them in tow. The horse darted aside a little way, and halted, checked.

Vincent rose, caught up the saddle bags, flung one glance at the pursuing figure of Durant, then was darting with his load across a bridge of corpses. Running, pitching, jumping, boots into face or back or thigh. Once across, he sprang from corpse to corpse. Not all dead, those bodies. Some of them screamed out or writhed as the leaping man shoved them down.

Durant spoke to his horse, panted out words, clung to the saddle. The other pistol was there in its holster. He caught at it, steadied himself; he had little use of his left hand, the whole arm was numb and streaming blood. One hand was enough. After a moment he left the horse and turned to the stream.

Vincent had disappeared in the swampy growth beyond.

DURANT FOLLOWED by the same deathly bridge, for there was no other. Whether firm ground or swamp lay beyond, was hard to say. Some of the corpses had sunk of their own weight. To one side, a Mexican, sunk to the hips, was screaming frantically for help. Durant went on, eyes ever seeking the one face, the one form.

Presently he saw it. A wide, pleasant little opening covered over with fresh new short grass, apparently firm. But there stood Vincent, wresting desperately at legs and feet—in the midst of it, held fast, sinking. That paled face, as he turned it, took Durant back many a year. It was the frightened, appealing countenance of a little boy; of Vince, the little brother of Tennessee, ere time and evil had branded it with the devil's irons.

Durant halted, testing the ground carefully, unable to go farther. He was not to be thwarted now by senseless compassion. But—shoot a fettered Vincent? It was too much like horse and lance against a naked man.

"Throw off those saddle bags, you fool!" called Durant sharply. Vincent sent a hasty frightened glance, tried to pull his legs from the sucking anchorage. "Hear me? Throw them in front of you. Hoist yourself on them!"

Vincent obeyed. He was gasping in air, shaken by sobbing breaths. He threw down the bags and tried to kneel on them, but could not. He propped himself with his hands on the bags and strained, doubled over, to free his feet.

The bags yielded, tilted, gradually gave. His hands were buried to their wrists. In wild alarm he broke them clear, before his arms were rooted. He had sunk over his knees, almost to his thighs. He turned his face again, a curiously blanked face. His voice had lost its mockery.

"Get your horse! Throw me a rope!" he cried out. "Damn you, Gordon—"

Durant stood motionless. He was quite helpless to aid. Even a rope would have been of no avail. He himself had to keep in motion, lest he sink—and Vincent was in quagmire a thousand times worse.

"Trail's end," he said calmly, coldly.

"Damn you! Lug over some of those bodies—"

"No use," said Durant. "And I don't intend to perish with you. Here's the best I can do for you."

He was carefully, painfully, wrapping the pistol in his hand-kerchief, to protect and save the priming. Disregarding the oaths, curses, pleadings of the other man, he poised for the cast and made it. The voice fell silent, as Vincent reached out. The cast was true.

With a writhe and a twist, Vincent had the pistol. He tore the handkerchief away, with a glad snarl; the round muzzle bore upon Durant.

"Now, damn you!" he yelled. "Bring up those bodies—"

Durant stood motionless, smiling slightly in assurance, in contempt. The ooze was up about the chest of Vincent now. His breath came in great gasps, his eyes were staring, bulging, distended.

"You'll not waste the load," said Durant. "You haven't the nerve. It's the best I can do for you, and more than you deserve. Good-by."

He turned and made his way out again, and across the stream. A frantic, vitriolic voice followed him for a little, then was silent.

Durant caught his horse without trouble and with some difficulty clambered into the saddle.

He tightened rein and rode away. He did not look back. The shot came to him distinctly, a little muffled but quite clear. The crooked trail had straightened out and ended in peace, void of hatred, for hatred was now of the past.

THE CLAMOR of pursuit, slaughter, death had been followed by that of victory gone mad with cheers and lusty whoops. Cowering prisoners were being marched en masse, to the Mexican camp and dead were being pillaged.

Durant, having stopped a jubilant volunteer and got his wound strapped up, rode on to the striped marquee, inviolate and under guard. He found Deef Smith in charge, dank with mud and blood, but beaming.

"Ketched the feller, huh?" Smith jerked his head. "She's in thar."

Durant strode on into the tent. The flaps fell, shutting out the world of prance and brag and jubilation. He regarded none of the regal trappings around him, the gay carpeting underfoot; only Faith awaiting him there, a little tearful, smiling, lips quivering, eyes glorious and welcoming—

A long while passed. Then she drew away, flushed, broke into eager words. Swift question and answer, the gaps of time bridged.

"Not hurt, not at all," she said honestly. "Santa Anna was gentlemanly, really. But Vincent—he broke in, seized the saddle bags—"

"Never mind," said Durant. "The gold doesn't matter, my dear. It's gone, with him."

"Gone?" Her eyes widened. "But you don't understand! It's here—in those saddle bags yonder!" and she pointed. "The ones Vincent took had Santa Anna's medals and his silver table service and some other things—I saw them all packed here."

Durant swallowed hard. "What? Then—then the gold—"

"It's here, yes; it was kept under the bed yonder. It's yours,

Gordon, all yours. It belongs to you and you must have it. Why, it'll make all the difference—"

Durant grimaced. "I don't know. Come along; we'll take the bags to Houston and leave the matter up to him."

So, with the weighty bags flung across the horse and with Faith in the saddle, they went down from the field of slaughter.

The sun was setting, the air still rocked to the yells of victory, the shooting, the explosions set off on every hand. They were men gone crazy, these conquerors. And though Houston had fallen in a faint from his horse, his leg shattered by a musket ball, there was no sleep or quiet in all the camp this night. Bonfires, processions with lighted candles taken from the captured camp, powder set off in wild fusees of rejoicing, songs, drinking, fife and drum banging away.

Deef Smith was sitting against a tree, leisurely fashioning a razor strop for tanning. He looked up as Durant stood over him, and grinned.

"Ketched me a good one," he rasped. "Better one out in the grass. They ain't brung him in yet."

"Santa Anna?"

"Look him up tomorrow. After the boys sober off."

Houston was lying propped up, occasionally swearing at his bandaged leg.

"The young lady will retain the saddle bags in her possession, since they are her personal property," he dictated. "I've ordered that private property be respected. The twelve thousand dollars composing the Mexican war chest will be distributed among my unpaid soldiers. As for General Santa Anna, he'll be found creeping through the grass on all fours, dressed like a common private."

A good guess. It was a cringing little man in blue cotton blouse, bedraggled, cotton trousers, red worsted slippers, brought into camp on a horse carrying double. From the prison corral, voices welled up. "*El Presidente!* General Sant' Anna!"

A furor convulsed the camp. The men crowded around,

cursing, growling, hot for blood. Houston, who had been dozing, swore lustily at being wakened for such cause. Snatches of the history-making talk came to Durant and Faith, standing at one side, but she had only one thing to say.

"He tried to be kind to me," she murmured.

At long last, Santa Anna's opium box was found and he fed his courage. Houston was nibbling away at a dried ear of corn.

"Attacked you on the second day, after you had received reinforcements? The very time! The very hour and minute! How can you hope to conquer free men, sir, when their general's rations are one ear of corn?"

This Sam Houston had the gift of leadership. The men, volatile as children, broke into yells.

"Hurray! Houston corn! Divvy up, gin'ral! We'll plant it for a liberty crop!"

"Not Houston corn." The man rose to heights again. "Plant it as San Jacinto corn, that it may remind you of your own valor—"

Houston, the maligned, the misunderstood; Durant stared at him, felt Faith pressing on his arm. Houston, bolstered against the oak-trunk, powerful and dominant, blue eyes weary, bushed brows twitching from agony of the shattered leg, yet with firm lips and gaze pondering deeply.

A lonely man within himself, self-sufficient, a hard-willed man who welcomed enemies and did not bend to friends; a man after Durant's own heart, one to be pleased childishly by a trinket of appreciation.

"I'd like one thing," Durant said, later, when they were alone with him. "A grain of that San Jacinto corn for me and mine, to plant in this Texas you've made free."

"Well said." Houston's gaze softened. "A toast, sir—you can drink it in that champagne of Santa Anna's the boys are opening. May your Faith be as a grain of corn! Texas has need of a valiant breed."

So the trail ended.

SOME FACTS WHICH CONTRIBUTED TO "TEXAS SHALL BE FREE!"

IT MAY be asked who was responsible for the massacre of the Texans held prisoners at Goliad. The alleged signed articles of capitulation, on terms that insured final liberty, have not endured, unless they are buried somewhere in Mexican archives; Colonel Fannin's copy was of course destroyed among his other effects.

No matter what the terms, Santa Anna violated the usages of war. He claimed that General Urrea did not cite the terms to him; Urrea claimed that the surrender was at discretion. Vet by Mexican statements, Urrea asked clemency for the prisoners. "The response of Santa Anna to the recommendation of Señor de Urrea was a strong reproach showing displeasure, and at the same time bidding him not to tarnish his triumphs with ill-conceived compassion." Three positive orders, it is said, were sent General Portilla, commanding at Goliad, before he obeyed. Even then he delegated the job to a subordinate. Santa Anna based his order on a Mexican government decree of December, 1835, declaring that armed foreigners landing in the Republic should be treated as pirates. Fannin's command were mainly citizens of the United States.

Three hundred and seventy-one men marched to slaughter. Twenty-seven escaped by flight. The bodies of the slain were stripped and heaped on brush fires. In early June, Texans arriving at Goliad gathered the unconsumed bones and flesh, still lying on the ground, and buried all in pits. No markers were erected, however.

The Mexican force at San Jacinto is variously put at eleven to fourteen hundred; the Texans were about seven hundred and eighty. Houston reports the Mexican loss at six hundred and thirty killed, two hundred and eight wounded, seven hundred and thirty captured, apparently including the wounded with the prisoners. About forty Mexicans escaped from the field.

But just what the hell anybody actually *knows* is beyond reckoning.

H. BEDFORD-JONES.

H. BEDFORD-JONES

BEDFORD-JONES IS a Canadian by birth, but not by profession, having removed to the United States at the age of one year. For over twenty years he has been more or less profitably engaged in writing and traveling. As he has seldom resided in one place longer than a year or so and is a person of retiring habits, he is somewhat a man of mystery; more than once he has suffered from unscrupulous gentlemen who impersonated him—one of whom murdered a wife and was subsequently shot by the police, luckily after losing his alias.

The real Bedford-Jones is an elderly man, whose gray hair and precise attire give him rather the appearance of a retired foreign diplomat. His hobby is stamp collecting, and his collection of Japan is said to be one of the finest in existence. At present writing he is en route to Morocco, and when this appears in print he will probably be somewhere on the Mojave Desert in company with Erle Stanley Gardner.

Questioned as to the main facts in his life, he declared there was only one main fact, but it was not for publication; that his life had been uneventful except for numerous financial losses, and that his only adventures lay in evading adventurers. In his younger years he was something of an athlete, but the encroachments of age preclude any active pursuits except that of motoring. He is usually to be found poring over his stamps, working at his typewriter, or laboring in his California rose garden, which is one of the sights of Cathedral Cañon, near Palm Springs.

Bedford-Jones has written stories laid in many corners of the earth, but among his most popular tales were the John Solomon stories which started many years ago in the *Argosy*.